DEATH FUSE

Was the killer's murderous instincts directed against a newspaper editor or a retired policeman? Was his target a Government Minister or a royal party? Or had the double-pointed nails been intended for someone else altogether?

When the killer struck again, London experienced a reign of terror. Theatres were evacuated and people searched, and still the bomber struck. Could he be caught? Not until the last minute did the vital clue emerge—but was it too late to prevent a new outbreak of violence, this time aimed at the police squad itself.

DEATH FUSE

DEATH FUSE

by

MARTIN RUSSELL

MAGNA PRINT BOOKS
Magna House, Long Preston,
England.

British Library Cataloguing in Publication Data

Russell, Martin
Death fuse. - Large print ed.
I. Title
823'.914(F) PR6068.U86

ISBN 0-86009-373-5

First Published in Great Britain by William Collins Sons & Co Ltd

Published in Large Print 1982 by arrangement with William Collins Sons & Co Ltd London and St Martin's Press Inc New York

Photoset in Great Britain by
Dermar Phototypesetting Co. Long Preston, Yorkshire.

Printed in Great Britain by
Redwood Burn Limited, Trowbridge, Wiltshire and
bound by Pegasus Bookbinding, Melksham, Wiltshire.

CHAPTER 1

The package was ready. It needed only its outer skin: beige wrapping-paper from the hardware store in The Broadway. Swathing it neatly in a double layer, he Sellotaped the edges. When it was sleek all round, he picked up the briefcase.

It was the angled, executive kind, containing already a selection of documents. Adding the package to the contents, he dropped the lid and clamped the hasps, carried it with care to the scarred mahogany stand beside the door and laid it flat upon the surface. For a moment he stood in thought, his fingers resting lightly upon the handle.

Presently he returned to the mirror.

A couple of screws held it to the cream-and-cerise-patterned wallpaper. Brown marks like coffee-stains disfigured the edges of the glass, which was also cracked in a fairly straight line from north-east to west-south-west; visibility, however, was barely affected. Stooping, he examined himself in the relatively unsullied area below the line, with particular reference to his hair, which was thick and dark, parted low on the left side, groomed to perfection. Having studied it from several angles, he hitched his striped tie more snugly into its blazing white collar before turning to reach for the broad-rimmed spectacles lying on the table near the curtained window. Hooking them over his ears, he poised them meticulously on the bridge of his nose, stooped again to investigate the result.

Reclaiming the briefcase from the stand, he left the room, tugging the door so that it locked behind him.

Sebastien Racine was worried.

Although training and instinct kept the signs below surface, to those who knew and worked with him the ripples were unmistakable. It was not merely the fact that the Grill Room had been overbooked, troublesome though this was in itself. There was a complication. He had just received word of the imminent arrival of a Most Important Party—

seven of them, no fewer—on its way from a charity rock concert somewhere in Chelsea, confidently expecting to be fed and wined at a moment's notice. The problem would be surmounted, but at the expense of further minor perforations of Sebastien's peptic ulcer, to say nothing of the discreet upheaval that must be caused by the physical rearrangement of tables. The whole business would have to be implemented without interference with the enjoyment of those patrons already established and coming to grips with their prawns au gratin. It was going to be like reconstructing a major highway without delay to traffic.

Sebastien snapped a thumb and finger. An under-waiter slithered across, apparently on greased skis. In response to a murmur, he signalled to a more junior colleague: together they glissaded towards a screened-off corner and slid aside the barrier, filled the exposed space with a couple of tables from a recess, packed chairs around them, then traversed back to the servery for trolleys. Sebastien's stomach relaxed a little.

He paused at a table. 'Everything to your liking, Mr Ross?'

Twenty-seven years in London had anglicized his speech, but his manner remained obstinately Gallic. The gaunt-featured diner looked up from his asparagus soup. 'As ever, Sebby. What's the flap? The Unexpected Guest?'

Sebastien smiled ruefully. 'I'd hoped our arrangements would escape notice. But to a Scotland Yard detective...'

'Ex-detective. I just happened to be looking, that's all.'

'A habit which no doubt has embarrassed many an offender through the years.' Automatically, with casual deftness, Sebastien was adjusting the cutlery as he spoke, removing surplus knives, edging the condiments into better positions; it was a sublimation of his urge to talk with his hands. He inclined a little. 'The fact is, Mr Ross, we're short of tables. An extra party is on its way to us. It consists...' He bent further. Ex-Chief Superintendent Duncan Ross listened solemnly.

'Royalty, eh? That's inhibiting. But you've dealt with 'em before.'

Sebastien glanced around anxiously. The waiters were covering the new tables with linen. 'After due notice,' he explained. 'Not...' He searched for the expression. 'Off the cuff.'

'Treat it as a challenge.'

From the corner of an alert eye, Sebastien spotted a newcomer at the Grill Room entrance and straightened hastily. 'In three years,' he confided, 'I shall be living at my farm in Berkshire. Breeding pigs.'

'Instead of serving them with apple sauce. Keep an eye on that not-so-distant horizon, Sebby, and you'll be able to ride above all this.'

The new arrival gave his name as Masterson and said he had booked earlier, by telephone. Sebastien greeted him with pleased courtesy while sending a practised eye across the list to confirm in a split second that such was the case; then, dogged by Mr Masterson, he set off on a tortuous walk that took them to a vacant table for two in an area normally occupied by the guitarists of the group that performed on three evenings a week. Turning, he was discouraged though not surprised to observe a slight frown upon the bespectacled face of his client.

'This table's not suitable, sir?'

'I was promised one nearer the centre.'

Sebastien's ulcer administered a small kick. Annoyance was a factor. Usually they did nothing but pester for tables at the side. You couldn't win. He said smoothly, 'We've had some difficulty, sir, but I'm sure—'

'Not to worry. This'll do fine.'

'You're certain?' The head waiter cringed at his own hypocrisy. In response to further digital snaps, waiters leapt from all sides. Mr Masterson was settled into his chair, equipped with menu and wine list. 'May we relieve you of your briefcase, sir?' Sebastien suggested.

'I'll hang on to it, thanks. Some papers I want to glance at.'

'Of course.' Sebastien deferred instantly to the natural desire of an English solitary diner to submerge himself in paperwork over the tablecloth. From the corner of his other eye he perceived restlessness among a nearby party of six which included a junior Government Minister and a newspaper political columnist. Mr Masterson was engrossed with the menu. With a warning nod to one of his juniors, Sebastien slid away.

'Something to drink, sir?' enquired the waiter.

'Nothing to drink. I'd like cream of asparagus and the roast duckling.'

'Thank you, sir.' The waiter offered a basket of rolls. Taking one, Mr Masterson tore it apart, daubed a fragment with butter and conveyed it to his mouth with an appearance of stern abstraction. Taking the hint, the waiter withdrew.

Clearing a space on the table, Mr Masterson opened the briefcase. Its contents he spread about him like a choice of vegetables: a notepad, a clipped sheaf of documents, a flat, plain-wrapped package. From a neighbouring table, a young couple allocatd him a brief appraisal before returning to one another's eyes. Seemingly indifferent to the room at large, Mr Masterson arranged the items tidily from left to right, studied them for a moment, lifted the package and transferred it to a shelf beneath the table-top, as though using it as a pending tray.

Drawing the documents closer, he

flipped through them. His frown deepened. He went through them again, with results evidently as unrewarding. Opening the pad, he made a note.

At the fresh tables, a team of three was setting out cutlery, working swiftly and without clatter. From the other side of the room Sebastien noted their progress, and felt a relaxation of the knots in his stomach-muscles. He had already decided upon the parties he was going to re-locate upon their arrival. Provided they went along without demur, ample space would be left for the royal group when it chose to appear. Sebastien allowed himself some cautious optimism.

He should have known better. On the point of walking across to exchange greetings with the amiable Sir Basil Grange and his pretty wife, who were up in Town for their monthly shopping day and were always good for some news about Berkshire, he found his attention caught by the sight of the solitary Mr Masterson on his feet, explaining something to the waiter who had just arrived with soup. Trotting across, Sebastien found the man returning things to his briefcase while the dish-encumbered waiter hovered foolishly at his elbow, rolling his eyes. Gesticulating him aside, Sebastien assumed his most solicitous posture.

'Something is not to the gentleman's liking?'

'Your service is fine.' Mr Masterson's voice was deep and resonant. He snapped the hasps of the briefcase. 'Better, frankly, than my secretary's. She's left out the vital sheet. I have to go back for it.'

'How extremely unfortunate.' Sebastien cocked his chin. 'We shall be pleased to keep your table for you until—'

'That won't be necessary. Thanks all the same. It'll take me an hour, and by that time...I'll grab a sandwich somewhere.' Mr Masterson swung the briefcase beneath an arm. 'Sorry to mess you around. What do I owe for the soup?'

'Please.' Sebastien's gesture of deprecation had all the sweep and style of three decades of troubleshooting. 'We shall be honoured to serve you another time. Mr Masterson's coat?'

'I didn't have one.'

They escorted him to the door. Behind his attentiveness, Sebastien was estimating how best to exploit this sudden addition to his resources. The waiter, cherishing his tip, was mourning the loss of a yet more stupendous contribution to his personal fortune: single and reticent executives in the Masterson mould, experience had taught him, exhibited a marked tendency towards lavishness on the strength of fathomless expense accounts in the wake of a good meal. Still, the cash that had changed hands was by no means to be scorned, and all that it had cost was a wasted trip with a bowl of soup. In the backwash of Mr Masterson's departure he remarked to Sebastien, 'That secretary's not going to fancy her luck when he gets back to her.'

'Probably they're lovers,' Sebastien replied absently.

'What difference?'

'It means that *she* will blame *him* for distracting *her*, so that she forgot to insert the draft contract.'

'How'd you know it was a contract?'

'It's always a contract.' Sebastien gave a soft clap of the hands. 'Don't let us waste time. Lord Kingsley and his guest will be wanting their main course, and Mr Masterson's table must be cleared and re-set. For two. The Bradley-Davisons can be accommodated there.'

'Good thinking,' applauded the waiter. 'That pair wouldn't know any different if we parked 'em by the kitchen ovens.'

Returning to the table, he retrieved the bowl of cooling cream of asparagus before turning his attention to the nearby Lord Kingsley and his latest bird, a truly devastating creature with wide eyes beneath a blond fringe. The previous week she had occupied the centre spread of the *Daily Scanner*, contriving in a variety of poses to make the latest winter wear for women look sexier than the most abbreviated of undergarments. They made, thought the waiter sentimentally, a more than presentable couple: a pity his lordship would be scraping the barrel yet again in a fortnight's time. He'd finish up marrying someone older than himself, with a squint. They always did.

'Who was the speed merchant, Barney?' enquired Lord Kingsley, indicating the vacated table with a nod.

'Fellow called Masterson, sir. He had to leave because he was missing some document or other.'

The young couple exchanged glances. 'We thought,' said his lordship, 'we saw him slip something under the table. A packet of some kind.'

'And,' supplemented the girl, 'we didn't notice him take it back.'

'Mind you,' smiled her escort, 'we weren't looking the whole time.'

Their gazes interlocked.

Beaming tolerantly, Barney paused on his way back to investigate the table. Sure enough, on the shelf underneath, partly hidden by the cloth, he found a package. Although a mere inch or so thick it weighed heavily, as if consisting of something like a stereo block. Displaying it to the young pair, who spread their hands in a self-laudatory way before returning to more crucial matters, he took the package across to Sebastien.

'Masterson left it. Under the table.'

'You're sure?'

'Kingsley and his piece saw him put it there.'

'He'll be back for it,' said Sebastien. 'Give it to me.'

Barney passed it over. It was while they both had their hands upon it that it exploded.

CHAPTER 2

The lift was out of order again.

A battered cardboard notice stuck to the door said: LIFT OUT OF COMMISSION. Direct from *1984*, reflected Cullen, heading wearily for the staircase. Mobility is Paralysis. It was much the same with the rest of the place: the interior walls, for example. Decoration is Desolation. Mushroom paint above bottle-green floor tiles. Silence is Echoes. Clashing doors, ringing footsteps. He added his own to the hubbub.

Most of his Squad colleagues were already assembled in the fourth-floor room that had been placed at their disposal by order, it was understood, of Whitehall. The room was oblong and large, with a view across to Westminster —if there had existed a window in the right place, which there didn't. The outlook that did offer itself was a blank wall of blackened Portland stone streaked with vertical lines of a whitish-grey as though someone had attempted to scale it in climbing boots and knee-protectors, and failed. Much of the room was occupied by a computer. The rest was filled with desks, telephones and, at this moment, a number of silent men.

They were gathered around a particular desk, examining photographs. Cullen joined them.

Somebody glanced up. 'Had your breakfast, Harry? Hang on to your stomach, then.'

Peering between shoulders, he gave the nearest print a long, steady inspection.

'Nail-bomb?'

'Only fifty or sixty,' said a dispassionate voice from the rear of the group. 'Sharpened, though. Both ends.'

'Thoroughness and efficiency.' Cullen kept his eyes on the visual record. 'Shows true dedication.'

He moved the uppermost prints aside, exposing others. 'What's the latest count?'

'Twenty-nine,' said the man to his left.

'No other survivors?'

'Just the one. The girl.'

'Very nearly the round thirty. Nice try, too bad.' Cullen turned his head. 'Chief in yet?'

'On the blower to A3.' His informant, a man in his mid-thirties with the build and stature of a cruiser-weight, ran a hand across his close-cropped gingery hair. 'He threatens to be with us shortly.'

The detective on his other side said earnestly, 'Got any hunches, Des?'

'I might have. If you want my opinion...' The voice of the ginger-haired man tailed off as he became aware of the glances being exchanged around him. 'Okay,' he said, walking across to a desk. 'You don't want an opinion. I'll keep it to myself.'

'Put it in writing, Desmond,' Cullen said on a note of encouragement. 'The Chief'll want anything he can get.'

'Sure he will.'

'Now we've upset him,' said the man who had put the original question, moving closer to Cullen.

'He'll recover. He works better when roused.' Cullen glanced up from the prints. 'What's your theory, Bob?'

The other shook his head. He was tall

and blond-haired, with a demeanour of tired alertness that suggested an active brain starved of essential oblivion. 'Early days for theories.'

'Personally,' said Cullen, 'I don't care for the smell of it. There's a definite—'

A door near the head of the room slipped aside. The group of seventeen detectives came intangibly to attention; turning his back upon the photographs, Cullen leaned against the table, facing the short, stocky man who had entered and was taking up a lecturer's position alongside a raised desk in front of a window rendered opaque by a cream venetian blind which stood badly in need of dusting. Somebody slid the door back into its groove.

'Right. You've seen the pictorial evidence.' The Chief's voice was unemotional. 'Any comments?'

He surveyed the room. Although he possessed no dominant physical feature of any kind, authority was built into him as style is engineered into a racehorse. After barely a second's pause he added, 'A3, for your information, are working on the political assumption.'

'Smart lads,' said a voice.

'It's the obvious inference, of course. One of the victims was the Under-Secretary of State for Foreign Affairs, with special responsibility for the Palestinian problem. Which speaks for itself.' The Chief blinked mildly at several faces.

Cullen said, 'Was he dining alone, do we know?'

'According to the editor of the *Custodian*, he was with Stephen Spelman, that newspaper's political columnist. Which raises the second possibility that our bomber didn't care much for the colour of Spelman's opinions. On the other hand, a couple of lords were among the casualties. Our chaps could be anti the aristocracy. Again...'

The blond detective next to Cullen said, 'Or a Royalty nut?'

The head of the Chief took on a tilt. 'Another half-hour,' he agreed, 'and the royal party would have been at table. The question is, though, could our man have known this? From all accounts, their proposed visit was a sudden whim of Her Highness's. The Grill Room itself wasn't notified until the last minute.'

'Worth a check,' said the ginger-haired man from his desk.

'I agree, sir, with Sergeant Ferguson,' said Cullen. 'The restaurant may have been the last to know...but the dinner party, and the rendezvous, for that matter, *could* have been mooted in royal circles some time previously. And somehow got leaked.'

'Check it out, then. Next, we have the presence—the not uncommon—of ex-Chief Super Ross. He dined there quite often, made no special secret of the habit. His movements could have been studied.'

'By a cop-hater,' suggested the detective occupying the desk nearest the Chief. Somewhat older than the rest, he had joined the Squad at a relatively late stage in an uneventful career, in the course of which promotion had peacefully eluded him. His particular aptitudes were serenity, a gift for liaison, and the infinite capacity for dogged pursuit of a line of enquiry to the apparent exclusion of the necessity to eat or drink.

'By someone with, as Detective-Constable Butterworth pithily indicates, no love for the Law. All these,' the Chief said equably, 'are possibilities that have to be kept in mind. With the political factor as current front-runner.'

The ginger-haired Ferguson stirred in his chair. 'Any warning phoned through to the Grill Room?'

'None, evidently.'

Others took up the theme. 'Not typical of the Irish. They normally go through the motions.'

'How about a splinter-group?'

'That meant as sick pun?'

'Breakaway mob, then. Not tied to ground rules.'

'Who do we know of,' enquired the Chief, 'that specializes in delayed-action bangers with twin-pointed nails?'

'It has to be someone,' said Ferguson, 'with an outstanding knowledge of explosive devices.'

The Chief bent upon him a look that brought to his features a hue resembling that of his thatch. 'A solid conclusion, Desmond. We won't argue with that.'

Cullen hid a smile.

'Whitehall's instructions,' the Chief proceeded, without emphasis or inflection, 'are that those responsible for last night are to be brought to justice at any cost. I leave you, gentlemen, to interpret those terms of reference as best you may. My one request is that you push ahead without delay, the lot of you. Milk your contacts: chase everything.' He paused. 'I think we can reasonably expect some help on this one. There must be many a villain with an ear to the ground who jibs at what happened last night.'

The detailed briefing that followed took forty minutes to complete. 'And bear in mind,' the Chief concluded, plaintively, 'that I want regular reports, not the occasional hint. I'd like a word with Inspector Royce, please.'

Cullen's blond colleague paused on his way out. 'Special assignment,' he muttered. 'Ain't I the lucky boy?'

'Some people have all the breaks.' Cullen clapped him on the arm. 'Be in touch later, Bob. Give my love to the AC.'

Royce walked over to the Chief's rostrum. 'Sir?'

'I'd be glad, Bob, if you'd go and talk to the survivor.'

'I thought Special Branch had done that?'

'They have, but it seems she was still a bit fuzzy at the time. Anyway I'd be happier if you saw her yourself.'

'Fashion model, isn't she? Girlfriend of Lord Kingsley.'

'Who wasn't so lucky himself.'

'How come she got out alive?'

The left hand of the Chief performed a graphic orbital flourish. 'One of those freak occurrences. She must have been half-sheltered by a pillar. By now she should be coming out of sedation. If the doctors will let you through, she could have something to tell. See what you can get out of her.'

'A couple of minutes,' said the staff nurse, sternly.

Royce told her that was all he needed. He walked soundlessly the length of the cushion-tiled corridor to the first of the swing doors. The uniformed constable who was stationed outside moved to block the way.

'You wouldn't be Press?'

Royce showed his credentials. Apologetically the constable moved aside. 'We've had 'em clamouring, sir, so I thought I'd better check. The doc says she's in no state to—'

'Quite right.' Royce pushed his way inside.

The room was divided from the main ward by a folding screen with glass panes let into the top. Approaching the bed, he stood looking down silently. The bandaged head on the pillow shifted inquisitively, the movement being accompanied by a slight heaving beneath the bedclothes. Pulling forward a chair, he lowered himself into it, inducing a leathery creak.

'Feel up to talking?'

The flesh crinkled between the bandages. 'I thought no one was ever going to ask.' Her voice was weak but controlled. 'Lying here like a zombie while everyone creeps about... Are you the guy that was here before?'

'No. That was someone else.'

'He sounded dishy. Still, you don't sound so bad yourself. Your voice reminds me of Gene Kelly or someone. Light and husky. They turn me on, voices like that. What are you here for, to learn all the gory details?'

'The preliminary part. The man who sat at the next table.'

'Oh yes. Your buddy was interested in him, too. I suppose that's why you came along. I don't remember a lot about him. Just that he arrived and went in...oh, a matter of minutes. Fastest Feeder in the West.'

'Can you describe him?'

'Male, Caucasian...isn't that the jargon? Fairly tall, good build. Dark. A great mop of dark hair.'

'Age?'

'I'm lousy on ages. Around forty? Lionel thought he looked like a merchant banker. How is Lionel?'

'Making headway,' said Royce. 'Can you tell me any more about this man?'

'I wasn't taking that much notice.'

'But you did see him put a parcel on the shelf under the table?'

'Yes, he did it quite openly. He had papers from his briefcase scattered all round him, so I naturally assumed he'd put the package there to make more room.'

'How long was he actually studying the papers?'

The girl lay thinking. Something caught in her throat and she gave a little gulp and a cough. 'Just the few minutes he was there. The waiter had barely arrived with the soup when he stood up and started collecting his things...'

'What reason did he give for leaving?'

'According to the waiter, he mentioned something about a document his secretary had forgotten to give him.'

'While he was working on the papers,' said Royce, 'did he wear glasses?'

'He had them on all the time. I think.'

'What type?'

'Thick-rimmed. Yes, they must have been. I probably wouldn't have noticed them otherwise.'

The staff nurse's head appeared round the door. 'Miss Clarkson ought to rest now. If you wouldn't mind.'

The bedclothes stirred more robustly. 'We were just getting along fine.'

'Plenty of time for chatting later,' said the nurse, briskly kind.

'By that time all these super men will have vanished. How long before I can see

Lionel?'

'Get those bandages off first,' said Royce, returning the chair to its former position. 'Thanks for your help, Miss Clarkson. What do your friends call you? Trisha? I once had a spaniel called that. She was a good-looker, too. Must be a good-looking name.'

'What a lousy compliment,' said the girl. 'But it was sweet of you to try. Come back if you want to know any more. Come back anyway.'

In the corridor, Royce told the nurse, 'I'm afraid we'll have to keep our chap on the door for the time being.'

CHAPTER 3

Miss Manning had been active in his absence.

The hearthrug was creased at one corner, and ugly square vase at the rear of the table had been shifted a little to the right. Also, the scooped side of the metal ashtray now faced the window instead of the fireplace.

Placing the carrier bag inside the crater of the armchair cushion, he closed and bolted the door before removing his coat and suspending it carefully from a wire hanger hooked to a nail protruding from the centre panel. From the right hip-pocket he extracted a small brownpaper parcel which he added to the carrier's contents.

On the windowsill stood a transistor radio. Drawing the thick, green velvet curtains across behind it, he flicked the 'on' switch, adjusted the tuning until Schubert's 'Trout' Quintet was coming through, clear and compelling, from the South Bank. For a few moments he stood listening, his head nodding to the lilt.

An alien whistle intruded. Wincing, he tuned it out, stood with finger and thumb on the control knob until the sound was free of interference; then, moving away to a green-painted cupboard which stood on fat legs in a corner, he took out a jar of instant coffee granules, an open bag of brown sugar and a packet of powdered creamer, which he carried to the table. On top of the cupboard stood an electric kettle. Filling it at the tap above the crazed sink bracketed to the wall between the window and the lumpy single bed at one end of the room, he plugged it into a power socket near the cupboard and switched on.

A blue china cup stood inverted in a matching saucer beside the kettle. Reversing the cup's position, he deposited two-thirds of a spoonful of coffee granules at its base, added half a spoonful of sugar. The kettle began to sigh.

The floor started to vibrate. A creak

from the landing was followed by a pause, chased in turn by a triple rap on the door-panelling. Switching off the kettle, he walked across, freed the bolt, pulled the door open.

Miss Manning was wearing her smile. 'Thought I might catch you at home. I looked up the programmes and I saw they were broadcasting some Schubert and I know you're quite fond of anything by Schubert so I guessed it might be one of your 'in' nights. And I was right, wasn't I?'

'Perfectly correct.'

'Nice, isn't it, when you get the tuneful bits.' She wagged a finger in time to the third movement. 'Music's a great comfort, they say. Especially when you're by yourself.'

'Do you want the rent, Miss Manning?'

'I really came up to say, if you're cold, don't forget there's a stock of fivepenny pieces for the meter downstairs in my kitchen, you've only got to tap. Only you need some heating this weather and though I always say it's a warm house, substantial, no draughts, still it's not quite like one of these modern insulated places, all fibreglass and such like, this is why I had the meters put in, you see, I don't like to think of anyone... Friday already, is it really? Whatever happened to the rest of the week? While I'm here, I suppose I could take the rent off you if you've got it handy, saves getting in a muddle over it, doesn't it, though if you...'

She watched him produce pound notes from a pocket. They vanished into her raddled fist like magnetic tape being sucked in by a computer.

'Don't forget, there's a stock of five-penny—'

'You'd better check that.'

'When there's trust between parties,' Miss Manning said primly, 'there are certain things the need doesn't arise for. I'll leave you to enjoy your concert, Mr Wood. What a cheerful piece that is, quite makes you want to dance. Well, I'll be getting back to the cooker, must have a meal for Mr Collins on the first floor when he comes in or there'll be ructions, nice to have a chat with you, bye bye for now and do keep warm.'

The landing floorboards groaned. He watched her to the top stair before shutting the door.

When the vibrancy had stopped, he re-shot the bolt.

The kettle took another minute to come to the boil. Before doing so, it generated a sustained howl. He increased the volume of the 'Trout' Quintet, and when the rival noises had expired he kept it as it was while he wrenched open a packet of shortcake biscuits from the cupboard and made the coffee. He carried cup and biscuits to the table.

From the carrier bag he extracted a number of items, including the brown paper bag which yielded a coil of copper wire. Lifting the lid of a rectangular cardboard box, he took out one of the double-pointed three-inch nails that were packed inside it in rows, each of them bearing recent file-marks. The box contained about a hundred. Holding it up to the light, he inspected the nail critically before replacing it with the others. Then he unwrapped another package.

For the next ninety minutes he worked assiduously.

The atmosphere was getting hotter, the music louder, the beat more frenzied. Secretly, Julie Morris had had sufficient.

Her skin felt messy, her calves ached, she wasn't thirsty but her throat was arid, and, worst of all, the inane witticisms of Roger and his vacuous mate from the assembly floor, Len Somebody, were beginning to stun her into a kind of aural dyslexia. There was no room to dance separately, as she preferred, and every time she ventured into the crush with either of them she felt on the verge of being raped standing up. The muscles of both her arms quivered from the effort of holding them off.

It might have mattered less if Diane had been showing signs of similar desperation. Clearly, however, she was enjoying the time of her young life. In view of the fact that simulated intercourse on a disco floor was as much as Diane seemed to ask of life, there was little sympathy to be expected from that quarter.

At the same time, an obscure sense of loyalty prevented Julie from leaving her to get on with it, and slipping away. This gruesome foursome had been as much her own idea as Diane's; to abandon it now, midway through the evening, would have amounted to recreational sabotage, besides wrecking their friendship. Even if she didn't mind if she never set eyes on Roger again, she wanted to keep up with Diane. There were times when she could be a laugh.

And other times when she was a pain in the...

Julie felt sick of the sight of swinging bottoms, the sound of thrumming drumsticks, the stench of beer, sweat, breath. She felt physically ill. Even Roger noticed.

'What's up with you, then? Gut-ache?'

'Feeling a bit wobbly, Rodge. Mind if I sit out a bit?'

'No, sure.' Irritation struggled with thin traces of concern in his voice. Detecting the concern, Julie reminded herself how kind he had been, that time in the works canteen when she'd dropped her egg salad and cheesecake all over the floor and everyone was splitting their sides: Roger had organized everything, even a replacement lunch, and in the gratitude of the moment she had decided she fancied him. If there had since been occasions when that had seemed in retrospect a hasty decision, honesty compelled her to admit that she had never yet felt strongly enough about it to act upon the suspicion.

'I'll sit over there a minute,' she told him.

'Like a drink?'

'No, thanks.' Her stomach rose and fell. 'Don't you stop. I'll be okay.'

Diane shimmied into range, showing her teeth and a lot of thigh. Roger, brightening, pursued her into the mêlée. Julie headed for a vacant bench.

On impulse she switched direction and made for the exit. While she wasn't planning to abscond, she felt no special obligation to stick around watching Roger leering at Diane's whirling teenage body and Diane sparkling back at him in the way that only the Dianes of this world seemed able to sparkle... Julie had tried it at home in the full-length mirror, and the effect hadn't been quite the same. A brief turn on the pavement, fourteen steps above, might do her no harm. By the time she came back inside she might be feeling better, and Roger might have stopped goggling at Diane and be waiting for her with that affectionate look he sometimes let into his eyes. It was worth a try.

For mid-November it wasn't a bad night. After the suffocating heat of the interior the street was unquestionably chilly, but for a minute or two Julie felt she couldn't care less if she picked up pneumonia. The breeze on her tortured skin was delicious. A few others were out there, couples mostly, refugees like herself: the difference was that they had each other for consolation. There was one other single, a biggish guy in glasses. He was leaning against the railings above the disco cellar, observing the street action, but not in an obnoxious way, more as if he was...well, just observing. A bouncer, perhaps, standing by for trouble. But somehow he didn't give that impression. He was dressed casually in Levi's and an anorak over a high-necked sweater, and there was a rolled-up newspaper—or possibly more than one—

under his left arm.

She wasn't conscious of drifting his way, but a moment later there she was within talking distance.

'Hot down there. I come out for some fresh air.'

'Crowded, is it?' He had a pleasant, deep voice. Not posh, but definitely a cut or two above some of the gutter dialects you heard in these dumps.

'You've not been in?' she asked.

'I'm wondering if I'd be allowed.'

'Why ever not?'

'They might think I was a bit long in the tooth.'

A closer look told her that he was older than she had thought. Well over thirty. She liked the dark wave of his hair.

'There's no age rule that I know of.'

'Does one need a partner?'

'Don't see why.' Julie had never thought about it. One came to discos with a friend, or in horrible foursomes. It was different for a bloke. He could please himself.

The man looked silently away along the street. Standing near, neither with him nor removed from his company, she felt awkward; it was like the conclusion of a job interview when you weren't sure if you'd been taken on or dismissed as a dead loss. To break what seemed to be an impasse, she said with more brassiness than she had intended, 'Why not come along in with me?'

He looked back at her. Internally she shrank, convinced that she must have sounded like the cheapest of tarts. What in the world had possessed her?

His appraisal of her was grave. 'That's kind,' he said eventually.

Hurriedly, without another word, she led the way down the entrance steps. The sooner she was back with Roger, the better; by herself she was apt to get into all sorts of scrapes. Not that there could be much harm in extending a helpful hand to someone too shy to shatter the ice himself. She knew what it was to be in that position.

While she had been outside about a thousand more people had apparently filed into the place and taken immediately to the floor. Neither Roger, Diane, nor Len Somebody was anywhere to be seen. Julie glanced back. 'Bar's over there,' she shouted.

The stranger at her shoulder looked where she pointed. He nodded. 'Thanks a lot.' His voice reached her effortlessly. He began threading his way towards the drinking area, the newspapers still clasped beneath his arm. Undoubtedly there was more than one. He must, she thought, like reading.

Julie had expected nothing. She hadn't fooled herself into anticipating any offer of any kind, that was for sure. Philosophically she turned away, stood on tiptoe, searched again for a glimpse of Roger's gaunt frame or the gyrating pelvis of Diane, but without success: the mass was too dense, the strobe lighting too hurtful to the eye. The group on stage were performing a number that involved a great deal of foot-stamping and guitar-posturing, punctuated by explosive shouts of an animal nature that Julie privately considered more appropriate to a jungle orgy. Such blatancy had the opposite effect to turning her on. If Roger and that Diane were revelling in it, they were welcome, that was all she could say.

Without having planned to she had backed up almost to the bar. For the time being it was doing little trade. One of the handful of people in its vicinity was the newcomer in glasses, who had provided himself with a glass of whisky, it looked like, and was standing nursing it while his gaze wandered about the place. In the course of its progress it touched upon Julie, spinning off again without a hint of recognition.

Resentment would have been childish. Perhaps he was extremely near-sighted. Certainly the spectacles looked strong, the lenses glinting in the intermittent glare from the stage; but they failed to give him the air of scholarly diffidence that might have been expected. On the contrary, he looked formidable. He held himself easily, and his shoulders forced the anorak into a powerful mould.

He wasn't the disco type. Julie felt a surge of affinity: she had just decided that she wasn't, either. She wished Roger would show up, so that she could tell him and discover his reaction. At this moment she spotted him. In a distant corner he and Diane were in close communion, partly shielded by passing figures, but far from hidden. A charitable interpretation of their joint activity was feasible, but Julie was in no mood for charity. From personal experience she was able to draw an instant and accurate conclusion.

She felt a little sicker.

These days, everyone knew, the idea was to be outgiving: to share, not hug people to yourself like objects. The odd thing was that the more she reminded herself of this the less she could bear to watch those busy hands of Roger's or the responsive squirmings of the sexiest girl in the typing pool, who had come along initially in the shambling company of Len Somebody, who had disappeared. No doubt he was in occupation of another corner, along with someone who had attended originally in company with...

Julie turned her back, convulsively, so that she was facing the bar and the bland expression of the bartender. He seemed to be scrutinizing her in full knowledge of the situation, taking pleasure in her distress. She thought wildly of taking the fight to him by ordering a drink, but her stomach rebelled.

The stranger, she noted mechanically, had finished his whisky and was returning to the exit. His example was a good one. Following, she saw that he was no longer grasping his bundle of newsprint: then she caught sight of it, protruding from a waste bin fixed to the wall at one end of the bar. At the end of the evening the bartender would help himself to the legacy, and good luck to him; he and the rest of them could do as they liked; she was going home.

At street level, the man ahead of her turned left and walked briskly away.

Julie came to a halt.

Indecision racked her. If she went off now, she was burning her boats, leaving Roger and that little bitch of a Diane in command of the harbour. Was this what she wanted? She couldn't be sure. She wasn't certain about anything. What she needed was time to think.

By now the street was almost deserted. Forty yards away a couple were waiting for a bus; they were the only people around. The stranger had vanished. With a dead weight clogging her chest, Julie leaned on the railing where she had first noticed him and stared wretchedly down at the turmoil she had just left.

Beneath her feet, the pavement shuddered to the amplified thud-thud-thud, keeping pace in a weird way with the oscillations of her mind.

For some reason, she needed to keep blinking.

In the riotous cavern below, a piece of electronic equipment malfunctioned. That was what it sounded like. It happened suddenly, as these things did. When her head had stopped ringing, Julie listened for the derisive shouts, the resumption of music at a saner level. She was vaguely surprised by the continuing silence, and the darkness.

The power supply, she thought, must have fused. That should give Roger and Diane plenty of rope, as if they needed any. Perhaps someone had done it on purpose.

With a foot on the top step she paused again, wondering about the silence. Then she heard the groaning.

CHAPTER 4

'Any luck,' asked the salesgirl, 'with the mice?'

'Two small corpses.'

'They say it's very good.'

'I'll plug it, any time. I'd recommend it to my landlady, only she'd never admit there was vermin within a mile of the place.'

'That's one forty-six,' said the girl, the tip of her tongue showing between her teeth as she wrote, 'plus thirty for the soap. One seventy-six altogether. Is she a dragon, your landlady?'

'She eats tenants.' He handed across a couple of pound notes. 'You suffer that way?'

She paused on her way to the till. 'How d'you mean?'

'With landladies.'

The girl's laugh was melodious. 'I live at home. Luckily. I don't think I could face up to some old crone investigating my way of life the whole time. Do you have the odd six?'

Finding three coins, he passed them over. 'Get on all right with your parents?'

'One parent. They're divorced. My father lives with this other woman over at Leytonstone.' Keying the amount, she produced change. 'Mother and I, we stagger along as best we can.'

'You earn the bread, she cooks it?'

'She can barely make toast. She has this fabulous job as assistant to a company director—she runs the firm, from what I can make out—but she can't scratch together a meal to save her life.' Again the laugh. 'Or her marriage. I'm convinced, the only reason my father walked out was because he was starving. Anyway, I now cater for the two of us. She brings in most of the loot.'

'Sounds a practical arrangement.'

'It works quite nicely.'

'Ever feel like a respite from the cooker?'

'Occasionally.'

'How about making tonight the occasion?'

'How?'

'Have dinner with me.'

She stared at the till for a moment. 'All right,' she agreed.

'Pick you up at seven-fifteen.'

'I'll have to phone my mother...'

'What does she do when you're not around?'

'She gets taken out by her boss.' The girl studied her nails. 'Or somebody.'

'Call her now.'

She hesitated. 'Okay.'

Waiting, he stowed his purchases inside the plastic carrier and then sauntered about, examining the stock. Freebottle and Sons was a hardware store in the old tradition, packed from floor to ceiling with devices for most conceivable purposes of humanity with the addition of a few that seemed to have strayed in from some other planet. An unguarded step backwards was likely to have serious consequences. With pocketed hands he was regarding a rack of secateurs and scissors when the girl returned, biting her lower lip.

'Fixed?' he asked.

'I'd better give you my address.' Taking a pad from beside the till, she started writing.

'Incidentally,' he said, 'I ought to know your name.'

She smiled faintly. 'Alison Duke. And hadn't I better incidentally know yours?'

'Lifting a pair of shears from its hook he inspected the handle. 'You can call me Colin.'

Unpacking the carrier on the table, he arranged the contents in size order before filling the kettle. When the coffee was made, he took the cup and the morning newspapers to the broken-springed armchair and began sipping while scanning the first of the front pages.

A picture, printed big, sprawled under a headline: *Disco Horror: Not Us, Say IRA*. The accompanying story he read with care, now and then frowning slightly over a phrase. Taking up another newspaper, he compared the treatments: it was the same picture, but the caption consisted of one word in giant Roman capitals: CARNAGE.

Rising, he went across to a shelf and took down a pocket dictionary, turning to the C's. *Carnage, n. Great Slaughter.*

He replaced the volume. Returning to the armchair, he picked up a third newspaper to read it with concentration.

At the end of half an hour he refolded all the newsprint and packed it into the carrier before rinsing the coffee cup in the sink, drying it scrupulously, restoring it to the cupboard-top beside the kettle. Letting himself out of the room, he descended the five clanking flights to the stripe-papered passage, lifted the communal telephone and dialled a number.

'I'd like,' he told the voice that answered, 'a table for two this evening.'

'And the name, sir?'

'Wood. I want one that's secluded.'

'All our tables,' the voice said coldly, 'give ample privacy.'

'If you say so. I'd like it at eight.'

He dialled again. 'Will you please send a car round to number thirty-nine Wallis Grove at seven o'clock this evening. Wood. Thank you.'

Back in his room, he bolted the door and drew the curtains before retrieving from the rear of the cupboard the brown paper bag he had placed there earlier. From the same storage place he took out a small hacksaw, a metal file, and a carpenter's vice which he screwed to the edge of the table, first protecting the woodwork top and bottom with a folded square of foam rubber. Untwisting the neck of the paper bag, he positioned it at a convenient angle on the table-top and pulled out the first of the three-inch nails it contained.

Clamping it firmly, he removed the head with the hacksaw, then filed the blunt end into a point. Giving the other end an extra sharpening, he released the sliver of metal and placed it to one side, took another from the bag and repeated the operation.

The shadow of his own head, cast by the bulb above and behind him on to the ceiling, hampered his vision. Turning the table he took himself out of the light-line. Before starting on a third nail he re-examined the other two, giving further attention with the file to the tip of one of them until he was satisfied. Then he went ahead.

By midday he had completed thirty.

Bundling them inside several thicknesses of newsprint, he lowered the parcel into the carrier, added the vice and tools, and with a brush and tray from the hearth swept up the metal shavings from table and floor. Pushing the table back to its original position, he emptied the tray's contents into the carrier.

On hands and knees he examined minutely the area beneath and around the table before putting on his coat and quitting the room with the carrier in his left hand.

As he reached the ground-floor passage Miss Manning emerged from her door.

'Off out for the groceries, Mr Wood?'

Her gaze was fixed upon the carrier. He gave it a casual swing. 'Do you happen to know whether the library stays open during the lunch-hour? These are overdue.'

Miss Manning said she was sure it did. 'Not that I use it myself. Should read more, I suppose, but then I never get the time. You like your books, I expect. It's nice, when you're by yourself, getting wrapped up in a story.' When she essayed her smile, the eyes above it became almost submerged by the flesh that billowed upwards from the twin areas between which her nose stood out like a cone-shaped volcanic islet. 'Quite good for fiction, aren't they, the libraries? Though better still perhaps if it's reference books and suchlike you're after, biographies and that, which a lot of people seem to prefer and I must say I can understand why, there's enough crime and violence to be read about in the papers these days without having more pushed on to you by people who seem to think it's their job to make your hair stand on end, though from all accounts that sort of stuff does go down a treat with some readers, twisted minds they must have, that's all I can say. If I was to make a guess,' added Miss Manning, continuing to observe the carrier, 'I'd say you was a travel man yourself. Would I be right?'

'You're a shrewd judge of character, Miss Manning.' He opened the street door and went out.

A walk of less than a mile took him to a fish restaurant where he had plaice and chips and a cup of thick tea, followed by a small iced tart with an almond-flavoured filling. While eating, he completed two of the crossword puzzles among his stock of newspapers and began on a third, but then returned them all to the carrier and sat back to gaze through the grimy window. A November mist had spent the morning struggling to lift. It was now admitting some debilitated sunshine, but its charity would soon be exhausted. The other feeders in the restaurant kept their attention to themselves. There was a steady trade in take-away meals.

At two o'clock he returned to his room. Miss Manning had been inside, leaving the cupboard door slightly less flush with its surround than hitherto, and straightening the corner of the mat beneath the table where he had left it doubled under. Bolting the door once more, he got back to work.

'Mother wasn't best pleased,' said Alison, 'about tonight.'

'You mean she'd no one to take her to dinner?'

'Oh, she'll have managed. I was exaggerating rather. She's not as helpless as all that. She can cook an omelette. It's just that... Well, one or two of her favourite TV programmes are on tonight and she likes to have someone to watch them with.'

'She could invite a neighbour.'

'She's quarrelled with all of them.'

Alison sat back to allow the waiter to serve the roast lamb. The intent look on her face gave her an appearance of vulnerable severity.

He said, 'I'm starting to have qualms about your mother.'

'She's all right.'

'The waiter came back with vegetables. When they were both served and had been left alone, he put a question across the table. 'I can't be the only person to have taken you out lately?'

Unembarrassed, she shook her head. 'You're not. The last one arrived on a motor-bike. I rode pillion to this pub on the A40. It was full of louts in leather. On the way back we had a puncture. Afterwards I went down with laryngitis.'

'You're safe with me. I don't ride a motor-cycle.'

'What *do* you do? I had a bet with Mr

Freebottle that you write songs.'

'I look like a songwriter?'

'I've never seen one,' she admitted. 'It was just something to have a bet on. I suppose now you're going to tell me you're a hod carrier on a building site.'

'Would it make a difference if I did?'

'To me? Yes. I expect I'd feel snobbish about it. I'm nobody to talk,' she added, looking and sounding earnest. 'A shop-girl who works all day Saturdays. My school chums would sniff if they could see me. Mother thinks I could do better, but I like it where I am. Old Mr Free-bottle's a sweetie. We have some laughs.' She sawed off a forkful of lamb. 'You still haven't told me what you do.'

'I don't do anything much.'

'You're a writer,' she said, decisively.

'What makes you say that?'

'If you don't write songs, you must be in the middle of some enormous novel. Or you paint. You've got a studio some-where.'

'Nice idea. You seem convinced I've a foot in the arts.'

'Well, you obviously don't do a nine-to-five job. You come into the shop at odd times. I've got it,' she said suddenly. 'You're a sculptor. All that stuff you buy —nails and things. You work in wood and metal. That *must* be it.'

'Okay, let's call me a sculptor. How long have you been with Freebottle's?'

She did calculations over her plate. 'About a year and a third. I'm twenty-two,' she volunteered. 'How old are you?'

'Older than that.'

'I'd put you at thirty-four.'

'Would you?'

She sighed. 'I can see when I'm getting nowhere. Awfully nice here, isn't it? Have you been here before?'

'Once or twice. I don't know it well.'

'It's a wonder they didn't frisk us as we came in. Some places are doing that, apparently.'

'Why?'

'Because of the bomb scare,' she said, her eyes widening.

'Oh, that.'

'According to the newspapers, a lot of restaurants are taking quite strict precautions. But I daresay that's more in the central area.'

He glanced down. 'Maybe I should have offered my briefcase for inspection.'

'I'm surprised you weren't asked to. What would they have found, I wonder?' She eyed him with innocent speculation. 'A typescript? Next month's chartbuster?'

'Nothing like that. It's full of explosive.'

Her eyes lost focus as they gazed across the tables. 'Those bombings weren't they *dreadful?* The disco, especially. All those young people, enjoying themselves. It must have been a madman.'

'Must have been.'

'No warning, nothing. Can you imagine the horror of it, down in that basement?'

'One can try.' He added a spoonful of mint sauce to his meat.

'They say the police have spoken to a girl who may have seen the man who did it.'

'I read that.'

'She had an incredible escape. Left the place a few minutes before the bomb exploded. All her friends were killed, of course. It doesn't bear thinking of. I can't understand how anyone could do such a thing. I can't get into their minds.'

'Of course not.'

She became aware of his scrutiny. A little awkwardly, she gave attention to her meal. 'I don't know why I'm talking about it. It's not the sort of thing one can do much about. I just hope they catch him. Tell me about your hobbies, Colin.'

'I'm too busy to have any.'

'The way you talk,' she said disgustedly, 'you should be the most boring man alive. Why aren't you?'

'I'm a good listener.'

'Yes, you are. You're terribly good. You sit there with a half-smile on your face... Why do you smile?'

'Enjoyment.'

'What of?'

'The look of you.'

'It's just my normal look. There's nothing I can do about it.'

When they emerged from the restaurant, the car was waiting obediently on double yellow lines at the kerb. The tiny coloured gap-toothed driver inserted it and them deftly into the traffic flow, humming to himself. The night was cold and clear, with a hint of frost. A few people were leaving a cinema which was showing a horror movie. From a coffee bar, rock music spilled across the pavement and into the road like dense smoke.

'I enjoyed the evening. Thank you very much.'

'We'll have to repeat it.'

'Next time you must let me take you.'

'That won't be necessary.'

The house was in darkness. She sat looking out at it for a moment. 'Mother's gone to bed. Like to come in for coffee?'

'No thanks. I'll be getting along.'

'You're sure?'

He said nothing. The driver gazed ahead. With a small movement of the shoulders she released the door and stepped out of the car, turning to look back inside. 'Well, you know where to find me. Next time you pop in, I'll have half a kilo of three-inch nails packed ready for you.'

CHAPTER 5

'At this stage,' observed Cullen, 'one high-blown theory is as good as the next.'

He waited for his change from the newsvendor at the mouth of Northumberland Avenue. Ferguson, a Tyrolean hat mantling his ginger bristles, gazed across the traffic at Nelson's Column. 'Papers don't think so,' he said. 'They're sold on the Palestinians.'

'They would be.' Pocketing coins, Cullen glanced at the *Evening Echo*'s front page. 'They might be right.'

'Somehow,' said Ferguson, 'I think not.'

Royce studied him. 'Got your own ideas, have you, Des?'

'Isn't this what we're paid for? Ideas?'

'Plus the hard graft that they entail.'

Ferguson consulted his wrist. 'In fifteen minutes' time, I've the first of three meetings fixed for this morning. I hardly think it can be said I'm dragging my feet.'

'Nobody's saying it, Desmond,' remarked Cullen with briskness. 'Let me know how you make out. I'm due to see a mate of mine, too. We've an assignation at Murphy's joint in Caledonian Road. He sounded breathy and portentous on the phone, but he'll have nothing for me.' Cullen shrugged. 'And yet if I pass him up... This girl, Julie Morris, who was at the disco. One of us ought to see her. She's been questioned, I know, but there may be some slack we can take up...'

'I'll do it,' said Ferguson.

'You're tied up till this afternoon. I don't want any time lost over this. Bob, how are you placed?'

'I can fit it in. You've got her address?'

Cullen supplied it. 'From the report I've seen, she gave a fair description of the guy she spoke to but couldn't pick anyone out from Records. Thinks she might know his voice if she heard it again.'

Royce seemed to be examining the outlines of the National Gallery. 'The other girl,' he said slowly, after a moment. 'The model. She told me the same thing.'

'So?'

'So why not bring the two girls together, let them compare notes? Could lead to something.'

'A big weep session, most likely. If you'll excuse me,' Ferguson said tersely, 'I've an appointment to keep. I'll check in later.' Turning away, he crossed the street at the lights.

'I know I should take him seriously,' Royce said, watching him go, 'but somehow...'

Cullen grinned. 'He does have that effect. At the same time, though, I've a feeling that one of these days he might surprise us. He's very single-minded.'

'He's surprised me once or twice already,' admitted Royce. 'I still can't bring myself to pay him the sort of awed respect he obviously considers he's entitled to.'

'I know just what you mean. Far as I'm concerned, though, if he should happen to bring home the goods on this one he can claim a gold medal and a peerage.' Cullen passed a hand across his eyes. 'Okay, Bob,' he added. 'I can leave Julie Morris to you, right? Exert your charm. From what I can gather she's in a bit of a state.'

The flat was on the fourth floor of a tower block overlooking the western side of Alexandra Park. The lift was out of service. Royce mounted a cement stairway inside a shaft of naked sepia brickwork to which aerosol operators had subscribed an assortment of messages and advice to the passing user. *Wogs Out. Spurs for the Cup. Death to White Bastards.* The interior of the Morris flat was a neat, almost luxurious contrast to its approach.

Julie's mother was thin-lipped. 'D'you have to bother her again? She's very upset. She's under the doctor.'

'Some of her friends,' said Royce, 'are under slabs in the mortuary.'

'I'll fetch her in,' said Julie's mother, after an interval.

The girl, clad in sweater and jeans, looked as though she had just emerged from a six-week confinement in a windowless cell and had not yet come to grips with daylight. The brown hair fashioned in a fringe just above her eyebrows gave her a baby-doll appeal that was off-set by the haunted appearance of the eyes themselves and her facial pallor. A little below average height, she was slightly overweight. Motioning her to the settee, which was upholstered in royal blue and festooned with small gold cushions, Royce sat beside her. 'I'm not here, Julie, to cause you more distress...'

'You are causing her distress,' said Mrs Morris from the door.

'Pipe down, Mum. I'm all right.'

'You look it.'

'Julie could be a help to us,' Royce told her.

'She's told your lot everything she knows.'

'I did answer a lot of—'

'I know that, Julie, and we're grateful. But we think you can help us further. You see, although it's reasonably certain you saw the man, you've not been able to identify him from our picture gallery of known suspects—right? But I'm told you think you might recognize his voice if you heard it again.'

'Not likely to, am I?'

'That depends. We might get lucky

and pick someone up, in which case voice identification could be valuable. Apart from that, there may be things about him that you've forgotten, but if you were given a nudge...'

'What sort of nudge?' came from the door.

Royce's explanation met with a renewed veto. 'She's not going anywhere else until she's—'

'Shut *up*, Mum. I want to. Now, d'you mean?'

Royce stood, extending her a hand. 'I've a car outside.'

On the way to the hospital, Julie said listlessly, 'It was me that invited him inside.'

'He'd have gone in anyway. You might just as well reproach yourself for not holding back every pedestrian who ever stepped out under a bus. Okay, is that settled? Now tell me something, Julie. This man, did he speak in dialect of any kind? Did he have an accent?'

After some thought she shook her head. 'He talked like a Londoner.'

'Well-spoken?'

She didn't think his voice had been any

thing special.

'A classless sort of voice?'

Julie looked blank. 'Middle-class, I reckon.'

'How about the pitch? High, low, medium?'

'Right deep down in his chest.' In quick embarrassment she glanced through the window. 'Probably why I took a bit of notice. That and the way he was just...standing about, like.'

'As if he was on the prowl?'

'Not like that. More as if he was waiting. Generally you can tell if a bloke's... you know. Out for excitement, like. He'd this sort of *calm* look about him.'

'When he followed you down to the cellar, he was holding something?'

Royce was still taking the girl through her account when they reached the hospital. Through the reception area and along the corridors Julie kept close to his side, liking and trusting this special copper with the steady eyes under rather untidy straw-coloured hair, the easy stride, the readiness to listen. She began to evolve a fantasy about him. Only to be jolted out of it when they reached a door with a policeman—uniformed, this one—seated outside, and Royce murmured with him before ushering her through, setting her pulse racing still more frantically from fear of what she might see.

What she saw was the patient sitting up in bed, bolstered by one of those purpose-built invalid cushions and with bandages about her head and neck. Her eyes were hidden, but not her mouth. Julie experienced relief. From its perch on a bedside chair a transistor radio was piping out some kind of comedy show. Hearing their entry the patient extended an arm, and, with only a slight fumble, lowered the sound.

'Not lunchtime already?'

'Feeling hungry?' enquired Royce.

'I might be, if I hadn't eaten haddock for breakfast. Hallo, I know that voice. You asked me some questions before.'

'This time I've brought someone with me.'

'Yes, I detected the patter of two pairs of feet. Listen, are you any closer to tracking down this maniac?'

Removing the transistor from the chair, Royce indicated to Julie that she should sit. He supported himself against the foot of the bed. 'We're making headway. How about you?'

'I'm doing fine.' The girl's hands, slim but strong, unmarked, were folded on the sheet. 'You can make out almost anything by listening, did you know that? When I asked about Lionel, I could *hear* their expressions.' The silence was a brief one. 'Somebody with you?' She turned enquiringly towards the chair.

Royce introduced and explained the presence of Julie, who murmured 'H'llo.' Trisha replied 'Hi.' Hesitantly, Julie put out a hand and touched the arm of the other girl, who responded by clasping her fingers.

'Seems to me,' remarked Trisha, 'we've both got a vested interest in the proceedings. What's he like, Julie, this sleuth you've brought along?'

'He brought me.' Julie gave him a shy glance. 'He's all right.'

'Good-looking?'

A nervous giggle escaped from Julie. 'I'd say so.'

'The handsome detective,' Royce told the pair of them, 'is running short of time. Can we get down to it?'

'What is it you want us to do?'

'Swop notes. You first, Trisha. Throw your mind back. Tell Julie everything you can recall.'

'Well now, what have we got? Biggish guy, well-proportioned, nice gear if you go for the square variety...suit, collar and tie, all the trimmings. Broad face. A mass of dark hair. Thick-rimmed glasses. How does that compare?'

Julie looked worried. 'The one I saw was more sort of trendy. Jeans and a windcheater thing.'

'Sounds as if he dresses for the occasion,' Trisha observed. 'Did he talk to you?'

'He asked me if he needed a partner to go into the disco.'

'Deep voice?'

'That's right.'

'Julie thinks,' Royce interposed, 'he came from the London area, by his accent. You go along with that?'

'I guess so. From what I heard, which wasn't a lot, he spoke standard English ...whatever that is.'

'Meaning there was nothing about it

that might help either of you to know it again if you heard it?'

Trisha said hesitantly, 'There *was* something. A sort of...deliberation. Right, Julie?'

She agreed immediately. 'Like as if he was watching what he said. Or the way he said it.'

'An assumed voice?'

They both nodded doubtfully. 'Not so much assumed,' Trisha elaborated, 'as an *alternative*. Are you with me? You know how some people's speech tends to vary, depending on where they are or the company they're in—or even what it is they happen to be talking about? I knew someone who, when he spoke about Wales, which he did rather a lot, suddenly developed this thick Welsh brogue ...quite unconsciously I'm sure, and it sounded perfectly natural. I mean he wasn't blatantly putting it on. He simply thought himself into the part each time, and out came this wonderful lilt from the Valleys. Actually he hailed from Suffolk. Maybe he had a split personality. Anyhow, I don't know whether Julie would agree, but that was how it struck me with this guy. As if he was subconsciously playing another role, so to speak, and the appropriate voice kind of came along for the ride.' Her head took on an interrogative slant.

Julie looked into space. 'It could've been something like that.'

'Don't let Trisha plant ideas in your head.'

'No, I think she might be right—honestly. It did sound as if he was using someone else's voice, even though...' Julie took a breath. 'It seemed to come natural to him,' she concluded, lamely.

Royce studied them both. While he was doing so, an orderly arrived with a tea trolley. He stepped back.

'We'll leave it there for now. I'll get you home, Julie, before your mother has fits.'

'Stay for a cup of tea,' urged Trisha.

'None to spare for visitors,' intoned the orderly, pouring a chocolate-coloured liquid noisily into a plastic beaker. 'Staff problems downstairs. If you're not prepared to pay a living wage, you can't expect—'

'Nobody expects,' said Trisha, holding

her free hand at the ready. 'Not these days. We're just grateful for anything that's flung to us.' Her fingers closed on the beaker. 'Sorry, Julie: refreshment banned. You'll have to get this incredible cop with the bedside manner to buy you coffee on the way back. Police funds should stand it.'

Julie gave the hand in hers a quick squeeze, and released it. She stood up. 'Hope you make out all right.'

'And you. Stay out of trouble.'

Royce said, 'I may be in touch again, Trisha.'

'You'd better be. Promise me one thing, though.'

What's that?'

'Catch him first, before he causes more damage.'

One the way back, Julie said, 'She's brave, isn't she?'

Royce gave her a sidelong inspection. 'How brave are you, Julie?'

Her heart gave a lurch. He was going to ask her to do something: inspect a line-up, perhaps. A row of impassive faces, staring into her soul. 'I dunno,' she said, despairingly. 'Not very, I don't think.

I've never—'

'So you won't be doing anything rash?'

'Rash?'

'Like going out at night by yourself for the next week or two.'

Her head shook, partly in relief. 'I'll not be going anywhere. Just to work and back.'

'What route does that take you?'

She described it. He gave a thoughtful nod. 'Sounds okay. Keep to that and you can't go far wrong.'

With a sense of terror she said, 'You reckon I might be in some sort of...?'

'I'm sure not,' he said promptly. 'But there's no point in taking unnecessary chances. Thanks for coming along this morning.'

'Did it help at all?' Her voice was faint and cracked; she seemed unable to keep it steady.

Royce stared abstractedly at the passing street. 'It may prove to have helped a great deal.'

CHAPTER 6

Having plumped the cushions and switched on the central heating, Ginny turned her attention to the cooker.

The steak and kidney pie was tanning nicely. She hoped Bob wasn't going to be late. He and the rest of the Squad had been working round the clock: for four days she had barely seen him. You'd think I was his wife, she told herself, instead of his kid sister. The most possessive of spouses could hardly have agitated herself more about the ludicrous hours he worked—not always, admittedly, but often enough to call into question the fairness of the system. Not that Bob would ever have dreamt of doing so. It's the same for all of us, he would have said.

Returning to the room they called the diner at the front of the house, she peered through the bay window along the street. For a terraced affair it wasn't a bad street to look at. A far cry from the riverside cottage she had occupied with Graham for fourteen blissful years, but she had a lot to be thankful for. The renewal of her grasp upon the purpose of existence, for one thing. She had Bob to thank for that.

And she was still only thirty-six. Time to re-marry, have children even. It was a thought to wrap about oneself, a supportive jacket. If it happened, well and good. She had no intention of getting worked up over the possibility. Perceiving the element of self-deception, she smiled at herself.

She gave a glance at her image in the half-length mirror, which Bob in a burst of domesticity had Rawlplugged to the diner wall, alongside the dresser. It showed her a small-built, compact woman with auburn hair cropped a little untidily into her face, large greenish eyes and a freckle or two. At this stage of the game she wasn't too sensitive about the sight of herself, although she had a few mild criticisms about which she had no intention of doing anything. Bob and her circle of friends seemed to approve of her as she was.

She did hope he wasn't going to be late. The framed citation for courage while on police duties had gone askew on its hook above the dresser; stretching up, she straightened it as best she could. She it was who had hung it there. Bob would have thrust it under his spare socks in a drawer.

She was back in the kitchen, salvaging golden pie-crust from the top oven, when she heard the rattle of the street door lock. With a lightened heart she placed the dish on the worktop and for the first time surveyed its contents as the work of art it was. Bob seemed to be making more noise than usual. Going out to the hall, she found two of them. Harry Cullen had been brought home to supper.

A wife, she supposed, would have rebelled. This was where a sister scored; she could experience surprise and pleasure without feeling guilty about it. She went down the hall, her smile of welcome produced without exertion.

'You've brought Harry. How nice.'

'Got enough for two of us, Gin? There

wasn't time to phone.'

'Luckily for you, I did go a bit wild with the ingredients. How are things, Harry?'

'Could be worse, Ginny.' He sounded drained. 'We could be at war with Europe. Look, if I'm causing you the slightest trouble—'

'Don't be absurd. You know we're both glad to see you, any time. Go through and fix some drinks while I get organized.'

'What will you have?' He was regarding her intently, straight-faced; she saw that he was too tired to smile. Her brother prodded him in the direction of the living room at the rear of the house.

'Come and take the weight off. I'll do the honours.'

'The usual for me,' she called after them, returning to the kitchen.

Suddenly the pie looked smaller. She poked at it anxiously, toppling a few extraneous fortifications, before transferring it to the food-warmer and turning her attention to the vegetable saucepans. Her movements were becoming fevered. She forced herself to slow up. When, five minutes later, she entered the living room, she was the competent house-keeper in full command of events and her own appearance; in the latter respect, a comb and some lip-gloss had helped. The pair of them were sprawled in armchairs, sipping Scotch. Her dry sherry was awaiting her on the low glass table. Before she could reach it, Cullen propelled himself across the room, swept up the glass and handed it to her.

'You're meant to be relaxing,' she reminded him. 'Return to the horizontal.'

'As the vicar said to the choirgirl.' This time he managed a grin before collapsing back into the cushions. His eyes met those of Royce: they gazed at one another with the apathy of shared exhaustion. Ginny perched herself on a footstool impartially between them.

'I needn't ask about progress.'

'Don't ask,' Cullen implored, with a groan.

Royce rolled a tongueful of whisky around his mouth, and swallowed. 'Somebody will talk. Eventually.'

'Bob's our tame optimist,' Cullen

informed Ginny. 'It's the sole reason we keep him on.'

'To whom,' she asked, 'do you refer? That man there? I'd almost forgotten. He's been here twice this week. Tonight's the second time.'

'My landlord,' said Cullen, meditatively, 'is convinced I'm losing a nightly fortune on the tables. He's a worried man. Soon he'll be asking me for six months' rent in advance. He has this twitch in his left eye.'

'Similar to the one in mine, I daresay, when I venture to ask Bob about his movements for the next twelve hours.' Ginny contemplated them both. 'And yet you both stick with the job. It beats me.'

Her brother lifted his right foot on to her lap. 'Some people prefer working unsocial hours.'

'What about those of you with wives and families?'

Royce squinted at the ceiling. 'Butterworth—he's married. He always seems to be among the first to volunteer for extra duty. Likewise Deakin.'

'Doesn't say much for domestic harmony.'

'But it's not just them. Take someone like Ashley Rowland, who's a fanatical spare-time photographer and secretary of his local society...he'd probably like more time to indulge his hobby, but when a job like this comes up he cheerfully takes his turn with the rest. Not just because it's expected of him: because he wants to. Des Ferguson, he's another one. He's fond of classical music. Given the chance, he'd attend concerts four times a week, I don't doubt. On the Squad you soon discover what's practicable and what isn't.'

'That's just my point. Why must it be the same crowd all the time? There must be others willing to take their turn at searching for sprats in the Atlantic.' When neither of them replied, Ginny added, 'Des Ferguson...He's the ginger-headed one who's afraid of women?'

Cullen blinked. 'What makes you say that?'

She laughed. 'He came here once with Bob, when they were en route for somewhere, and the moment I greeted him I knew. You can't fool Us Girls.'

'He's a reticent type,' Cullen conceded

'with a bit of a chip on his shoulder, possibly, but I wouldn't know about his sex life. He does live in a hotel room, so maybe you're right, he's happier being looked after by an anonymous chamber-maid. But then, eight-tenths of the Squad seem to exist in rooms of one kind or another.' He smiled at her. 'I dwell in a bed-sit myself.'

'An apartment,' murmured Royce, 'with resident porter, high-speed lift and entry-phone. Remind me to rough it some time. Supper ready yet, Gin?'

Facing Cullen across the table, aware of his slightly mechanical movements with knife and fork, she caught herself wondering about that apartment of his in Maida Vale. Did he keep out of it as much as possible? Since his divorce, such trivia as home comforts and regular meals would in all probability have taken a back seat. To date, Bob had told her, no other female seemed to have gained a toehold upon Harry's lifestyle. He was showing all the wariness of an amateur gardener stung by nettles; for the moment, horticulture had lost its allure. She felt a ridiculous urge to lean across her plate, ask him how he was managing.

'This is awfully good, Ginny,' he said, glancing up.

'I suppose you've both been existing on pints of beer and ham rolls.'

'The sandwich bars come in useful, I find. I can't answer for Bob.'

'I work better when I'm not eating.'

'If it weren't for his fuss-pot of a sister,' Ginny explained, 'he'd cruise along exclusively on air and inspiration. Until suddenly, to his great amazement, he'd find himself falling apart.'

'No chance of that,' Royce said with his mouth full. 'Not while you're around.'

'All I can do is repair the ravages from time to time.'

'You seem to do a good job,' said Cullen. His knife and fork came to rest as he pondered. Presently he went on, 'Getting back to what you were saying earlier, the alternative to people like us pounding the streets in search of those sprats you were talking about, is...what? Lining up a specimen cross-section of the population and having them shot? That might help solve the housing shortage. But there's no easy way of tackling a problem like this. You can't take short cuts. You just have to whittle away, hoping to God that at some stage, sooner rather than later—'

'If this is how you go on at mealtimes,' remarked Royce, 'I don't wonder Maureen walked out on you.'

Ginny sent him an appalled look. Cullen, however, grinned. 'I walked out on her. And sometimes it feels as if I've been walking ever since. Today especially.'

Passing him the potato dish, Ginny said venturesomely, 'Do you prefer living alone, Harry?'

'It has its advantages.' His look was friendly, but it warned her off. He turned to Royce. 'Remind me to tell you about another possible lead Pink Percy mentioned as an afterthought. I didn't think anything of it at the time, but on reflection... We'll talk about it in the morning. Do you have anything else to follow up?'

Royce nodded. 'One more call to make tonight.'

'You mean,' Ginny asked in dismay, 'you've got to go out again?'

'Just for an hour. It's to see someone I

can't get hold of any other time. I'll be back by eleven. Harry can stay and keep you company.'

'Perhaps Ginny would sooner be left in peace.'

'Ginny gets quite enough of that, thank you.' She tried to sound casual. 'Unless you're anxious to get home, why not stay for coffee and put your feet up? You're very welcome.'

'Hey,' he said. 'I thought I was the arm-twister around here.'

'So we bought this house between us,' said Ginny, adding cream to the coffee, 'and it's worked out like a dream.'

Accepting the cup, Cullen said, 'That's because you and Bob hit it off.'

'I expect I drive him round the bend, sometimes. He's very good at putting up with me.'

'He'd make someone a good husband.'

'If he wasn't married to his job.' She sat back with her feet up on the stool between them. The only light came from a standard lamp in a corner, and the room's muted glow seemed to invite confidences. 'He nearly did, once,' she added, noticing how, when he sat listening, Cullen's body seemed to tense and coil as if to absorb every nuance and overtone, like a radio receiver picking up signals.

'But he didn't go through with it?' he asked, when she paused.

'He'd have gone through with it. But the girl died.'

'Oh. That's tough. I never realized.' Cullen sat stirring his coffee. 'I can't make up my mind,' he said presently.

'About what?'

'Whether it's better that way, in a sense: or whether, despite everything, one ought to be thankful for having had the chance to develop a relationship. Even if it goes sour.'

'They say all experience enriches.'

He gave a short laugh. 'Enlightens, perhaps. I'm not sure that wealth comes into it.'

'That sounds a little bitter,' she suggested.

'Let's just say I'm marginally more aware than I used to be.' He sat forward, slopping coffee over the carpet. 'I know

now, for instance, that luck can be pretty erratic in its judgments...at least over the short term. Take yourself, Ginny. Do you think it's played fair?'

'I've had any amount of luck,' she said, embarrassed.

'The bad type as well as the good.' Leaning forward, he mopped the carpet with his handkerchief. 'Or is there an atom of difference between them?'

'You think they're a couple of impostors?'

'I think they both come under the same heading: something you have to fight against.' Sitting up, he pocketed the handkerchief. 'I've ruined your carpet.'

'It's the same shade. It'll merge in.'

He looked at her. 'I can see what your husband must have appreciated about you.'

She could think of nothing to say. Cullen hit the bulge in his pocket with a fist. 'That was bloody clumsy. I'm sorry.'

'It's all right,' she said, smiling at him. 'I don't mind talking about Graham.'

'Even when people are trampling over your feelings in hobnail boots?' Cullen leaned back with his hands behind his head. 'Was he a copper?'

'Lord, no. He was in boat-building. Motor cruisers. He had this small firm with premises on the river, not far from Staines.'

'Sounds fun.'

'He enjoyed it. Apart from...my own feelings in the matter, I always thought it was a bit harsh that, just when they were starting to make a go of it, he had to walk into that spot of trouble.' Seeing the lift of his eyebrows, she added, 'Bob hasn't told you?'

'Not in detail.'

'Well... What happened was, Graham was returning one night from seeing a potential customer at a pub in Staines—he was walking back to his car, actually—when these three youths sprang out on him. It was a side-street, rather dark. Graham was handy with his fists and he put up a good fight, but one of them hit him with a length of wood and knocked him cold. They took his wallet and ran off. After he came round he managed to stagger to the car and drive to the police station. Then he came home.'

Ginny fingered the coffee-pot. 'He seemed none the worse. A few days later, though, he started complaining of double vision and headaches. The doctor gave him tablets, but it got more and more persistent and eventually he went into hospital. It turned out there was pressure on the brain. They operated, but it wasn't a success. He died two days later.'

Cullen was watching her fingers. 'How far back was this?'

'Four years.' She relinquished the pot, gave him another smile. 'I married at eighteen.'

'Presumably they never caught the yobbos?'

'They did, as a matter of fact. All three of them were brought to court, accused of murder. They had a clever counsel, though, who managed to produce medical evidence that Graham had an exceptionally thin skull, and since they hadn't been in trouble before—or hadn't been caught—they were each given a suspended two-year sentence and fined a hundred pounds. So...' She took a breath. 'Justice was done.'

Cullen said nothing.

'At least,' she added, 'we did have fourteen good years together. So I've something to look back on.'

He was staring at her. 'As far as I can see,' he said, 'that makes it a damn sight worse.'

'I'm sorry?'

'That was no crime. It was an obscenity. People like that ought to be stamped out. Obliterated.'

'For a while I felt the same.'

'You still should.'

'If I did,' she said carefully, 'I'd forget the happy times, wouldn't I? They're more important to me.'

She put out a hand for his cup. Taking it, she was surprised to observe that his own hand was trembling. In the half-light it was difficult to tell, but it seemed to her that his colour had risen. 'That's my catastrophe,' she said, pouring. 'How about yours?'

'I've nothing to trade.'

'Make me an offer.'

'Christ, it's pathetic by comparison...'

'I'd like to hear.'

'It's not even as if I tell it well.' He

spoke jerkily. 'I was with a demolition firm. Maureen worked in accounts. We got married. Misguidedly, perhaps, I quit the firm and joined the force, then went on to the Squad. Maureen didn't care much for the hours that involved. She started looking for diversion. Found it with a local dentist. Became his assistant and they started an affair.'

'Did you know?'

'I guessed, but I let it slide. Thought it might peter out, and anyhow...' He paused.

'You were otherwise occupied yourself?'

'Not in the way you mean. Like Bob, I was wedded to my work. I suppose I was pretty stubborn about making no concessions to the needs of a wife, they seemed irrelevant to me at the time. Anyway, the outcome of it was fairly traditional. A civilized bust-up. After an appropriate lapse of time, the dentist lost himself an assistant and gained himself a wife. My profit was—what was it you said?—a hunk of enriching experience. In a way you're right. It did give me a healthy suspicion of dental surgeons.'

'I hope it gave Maureen a set of perfect teeth.'

'I wouldn't know, I was rarely given a sight of them.' He glanced up. 'Now that really does sound bitter. Maybe I should publish the paperback version, get it out of my system.'

'In the right market it could be a best-seller. That sounds like the return of the wanderer.'

Royce came into the room, switching on the main light and instantly dousing it again. 'Sorry. Wasn't thinking. If you two want to be left in peace in the half-dark, I don't mind crawling off to—'

'That,' said Cullen, struggling up, 'sounds like my cue, loud and clear from the wings. How did you make out?'

'I could have saved my energy.' Royce glanced from Cullen to his sister. 'Did I miss a good coffee-break?'

'You missed the script-conference.' Cullen gave him a slap on the arm. 'See you tomorrow, Bob. I'll let myself out. 'Night Ginny. Thanks for everything.'

'What did he mean by that?' Royce asked.

'About the script? I can't imagine,'

she said hypocritically. She began collecting things on the tray. 'Like some coffee? No, you'd rather get to bed. Bob...'

'What is it, Gin?'

'Oh, nothing. He's a bit screwed-up inside, isn't he?'

'Who, Harry?' Her brother looked perplexed. 'In what way?'

'Just in the way he looks at certain things. You don't think it ever affects his judgment?'

'If it does, we're all thinking down the same wrong lines.' Stooping to kiss her, he held her shoulders for a moment. 'In one sense,' he told her solemnly, 'I'd say his judgment was impeccable.' Their eyes met. She felt herself blushing. 'Good night,' he added, kissing her again.

'But then, you're biased. For that, you can take the tray outside and wash up.'

CHAPTER 7

In the normal way, the last thing Julie would have wanted was the company of Sheila Farrell.

In truth, she would have gone to some lengths to elude the creature. On this occasion, however, she was prepared to put up with her because of what the nice-looking detective had said about being out at night by herself.

Not that five-thirty, by any stretch of logic, could be described as night. On the other hand, the degree of darkness at this hour was undeniably much the same as it would have been at two in the morning, which in Julie's estimation was the conclusive factor. It was like saying that you needn't look both ways when crossing a one-way street. Cars had been known to transgress the law. And however irregular it was when they hit you, the effect was just as painful.

Sheila, a large lumpy girl with a bustline that filled most of the space between her neck and waist, and calves like air-port windsocks, was in no doubt of the absolute rapport between herself and Julie. It was a conviction of long stand-ing. Nothing that Julie could do or fail to do had ever come within a mile of per-suading Sheila otherwise. At lunchtime she would 'keep Julie's place' at her table in the works canteen; morning and after-noon she would time their tea-breaks to coincide; on Fridays it was rare that she failed to come up with a programme of suggested joint activities for the week-end. Up to now, only a strong and sus-tained rearguard action on Julie's part had to some extent held her off: that, and the competition from young Diane, whom Sheila had cordially detested. But Diane wasn't around any more.

Julie had no wish to think about Diane. In the accomplishment of this aim, she could conceive of no more will-ing ally than Sheila, to whom the mere mention of the name had always been the signal for a dangerous tightening of the lips. It was another good reason for her acceptance of the great blancmange as a fellow-traveller on the Tube this evening.

An unpleasant shock, however, awaited her. The moment they had found seats, Sheila gave tongue.

'You know, Julie, you're looking dead rotten. I was watching you today, while you was working, and I was thinking, how'd I be feeling if it'd been me, know what I mean? I think you're ever so plucky, coming back so soon after.'

'I'm not,' said Julie. 'I wanted to. Better'n sticking around at home.'

'Ooh, that's murder, stopping at home. No, what I thought, you might not've wanted to be reminded of the people you was with...'

'I don't.'

'I wouldn't, neither. Brenda and me was talking and I said to her, that Diane, I said, so sort of bright and lively she was, full of mischief an' that, then suddenly before you know what's happened—'

'How's Brenda getting on with her bloke?'

'Still knocks around with him,' Shelia replied vaguely. 'She was saying, the last time she spoke to Diane...'

The eyes of a man strap-hanging at the far end of the compartment seemed to be fixed upon Julie with a glazed intensity. To avoid them, she shifted in her seat so that she was able to look the other way without making a thing of it. A framed notice at the opposite end came into her line of vision. From this distance she couldn't read it: unfortunately, she knew more or less what it said. Something about what to do if you found an unattended parcel lying around inside the train. You weren't to touch it, but you were to get everyone to leave in an orderly fashion at the next station and inform the guard. Provided, that is, that your mouth wasn't too dry to produce speech. Badly as Julie wanted to dam Sheila's flow, divert it into remote channels, the task was physically beyond her. Panic crowded in. She had an overwhelming urge to leap up, jump from the train, run like a gazelle into open space. If she took off now, she would first shred herself on shattered window-glass and then dash herself to pieces against the tunnel wall.

She almost wanted to do it. In desperation she changed position again, gave Sheila the kind of close attention she must have despaired of ever getting.

'...never dreamt she'd finish up on one of them casualty lists you read about...'

The man with the glazed expression was tall and well-built, but he was very nearly bald and there was a kind of gingery hue to his face. He was just a starer. Normally, Julie could have withstood his scrutiny without effort. This evening, she felt like a thirteen-year-old enduring it for the first time. Between Sheila on the one hand and those codlike orbs on the other, there was little she could do except try to make her mind a void, and she wasn't too good at that, especially now. Please, God, let the train slow down and stop. The wheels lurched, their note altered; God had heard and answered. The balding man, she saw, had been pitched off balance and was apologizing to a neighbour. Almost immediately, however, the gaze re-established itself. Julie half-rose.

Sheila grabbed her arm. 'We're not there yet.'

'It's just pulling in.' Detaching herself,

Julie fought her way to the doors farthest from the man. Pursuing her like an immense flabby bladder, Sheila talked unceasingly. As the train stopped, they spilled on to the platform to be snatched up in the current drifting towards the Way Out sign, and Julie had time only for a quick glance back. It showed her the balding man still on the train. The doors rumbled together.

Relief struggled with the panic that was again assaulting her as the current slowed, bringing them virtually to a halt.

By the time they reached the escalator she felt ready to faint. Sheila, standing on the step below as they ascended, still confronted her on level terms. How could a girl so vast, so grotesque, retain an interest in living? By taking morbid notice of everyone else, that was how. Her voice bleated on. Staring upwards, Julie could see that the full width of the escalator was blocked to the top: it was the mechanism's pace or something. Someone of a malignant nature had switched it to quarter-speed. The man in the poster advertising Y-fronts had a mouth and a chin reminiscent of Roger's.

She hadn't noticed that before.

'...personally think she's wasting her time, same as Diane was. I mean if a fellah says that sort of thing to you, you don't just sit there, do you, and take it? Not if you've a bit of self-respect. But then like I've always said, Brenda...'

In the street, illuminated spears of rain were being hurled out of the night. Julie found a rain-hat and put it on. Practically dizzy with rapture at getting out of that hell-hole, she followed Sheila mechanically to the bus-stop and stood passively beside her in the queue, registering the words and erasing the meaning. The rain wasn't much, but the breeze was on the sharp side. She was glad of the two sweaters under her jacket.

Somebody jostled her. To steady herself she had to plant a foot in the gutter. A male voice said 'Sorry.'

Without glancing at its owner she replied 'Okay.' The voice had been thin, immature; she could guess at the face that went with it. Gaunt, with an irregular nose, a loose lower lip above a retreating chin: she had seen enough to last her for ever. There were times when it seemed to be the only model still in production. Which was why anything different stood out, grabbed your attention, like broad-shouldered strangers with deep voices...

Behind and above her, Sheila was gobbling on about Brenda. 'That's where she goes wrong, if you ask me. She's all right, she means well, but if you once get on the wrong side of her...'

The bus nosed alongside, chuckling to itself. Julie went with the drift, allowing Sheila to get ahead and haul herself laboriously aboard, at which point Julie stood back.

'Think I'll walk, after all. Feel like some fresh air.'

Sheila's amazed face swung about. 'Huh? It's raining. You'll get soaked.'

'No I won't. See you tomorrow.' Julie waved as the other girl was eased irresistibly into the interior and swallowed up.

The remainder of the queue swept past. Turning thankfully, Julie elbowed a path through the ruck, reached open pavement, trotted a few yards until she was clear of the stragglers, then dropped her pace to a quick walk. Raindrops stung her cheeks.

Freedom was bliss. Despite her fatigue, her longing to get home, she felt nothing but gladness at having contrived to break away from dreadful, overpowering Sheila and, just as vitally, the bulb-lit coffin of the bus's lower deck. From the station back to the flat was a fair step, but most of it was along the main street in the radiance of shop-fronts, and if she had taken the bus she would still have had to cover the final stretch by herself —because Sheila lived two stops back— through residential minor roads whose lighting had never been intended as more than a token.

The rain was really coming on. Thanks to the waterproof hat, her hair would be all right, but her jacket and slacks were going to suffer, and as for her shoes... She wished she was wearing a more substantial pair, like the person walking behind her whose footsteps she could hear above her own, slapping like wet plaice on a slab. Veering abruptly, she crossed the street at the pedestrian lights and gained some shelter from the overhang of the buildings on that side.

Her move achieved little. The sole difference was that the slap-slapping was, if anything, closer. Dodging a puddle, Julie used the excuse of breaking step to trot a few yards. When she slowed again, she seemed to have placed no extra distance between herself and that contrapuntal sound: it remained as persistent, as intrusive as ever.

A couple of cars hissed past. When they were gone, the street relapsed into wet apathy, like an exercised pet that knew it had been left to slumber for the night.

At the end of the shopping parade, a right-hand turn led to the estate. Three high-rise towers girdled by half a dozen four-storey blocks: peaks among foothills. From several directions roads reached in, concrete fingers probing. Crossing the mouths of two of them, Julie was conscious that she was proceeding almost at a lope. She couldn't bring herself to look back. Inside the shoes, her toes were sodden. In such conditions, nothing could be more natural than a wish to shorten the journey...any sensible person would have done the same, and the person to the rear of her was undoubtedly as full of sense as most. Naturally, on a night like this, nobody would want to loiter.

Straight into another puddle. She couldn't get wetter. Once home, she could strip off, change into dry crisp things; first, perhaps, sink into a hot bath. She had an urgent wish to be supine in steaming water, secure behind a locked door. Just a quarter of a mile—five hundred strides?—and she could embark upon the entire delicious process, taking her time. Listening through the thin wall to those prissy voices on *Nationwide* from the TV in the living room.

Between the street and the first of the outer blocks lay a litter-strewn grassed expanse. Then came a fenced-in rectangle of tarmac with a climbing-frame in one corner: the children's play area. Next to it, a kidney-shaped lake with protruding pram-handles; and next to this, an ornamental garden encased in stake fencing six feet high. Between lake and garden, a footpath enclosed by railings led off on a winding course towards Archie House, the nearest of the tower blocks.

Every twenty yards along the footpath there was a lamp on a column, but all of them had been vandalized. Some light crawled across from the street or dribbled from the flat windows, most of which were heavily curtained. Julie could see enough to keep up a smart pace, without actually running.

She didn't want to run. To do so might activate the footfalls behind her into a gallop. Turning off, Julie had hoped that the sound might dwindle away along the street: instead, the intensity of its beat had mounted, like the brushed-percussion accompaniment to a hit number, muted but insistent. A slight irregularity was detectable. Perhaps, she thought hopefully, it was a very old person, caught out in the rain and darkness, toiling to keep pace with her for the sake of company; in which case, she had been not only stupid but inconsiderate. It might even be elderly Mrs Radbone from Flat 24, returning from a visit to her single-parent daughter in Bingham

Avenue. The poor old thing was arthritic, and on a night like this...

Julie looked round.

The figure was thin and stooped, travelling in a lurching shamble. In nightmares, Julie had often coiled herself into a ball to evade the claws clutching for her...only to find herself rolling unstoppably downhill into their reach. She had the same feeling now. As she tried to flatten herself against the railings, they seemed to be pushing her out, directly into the path of the oncoming horror. Above the slapping leather and the swish of moisture she could hear a faint gasping noise, suggestive of excitement. Her limbs were locked. She had a strange exterior view of herself, seen from above. She was crouched in an alley, arms about her head, waiting dumbly for disaster. She ought to call out. Why didn't she move, shout, do something?

Something brushed her arm.

'Sorry...'

The word reached her in a mumble. The railings were at her back, biting into her shoulder-blades. Her eyes remained open but she could see nothing. She tried to scream. Her throat refused its help.

The slapping beat was softer, dying away. Suddenly she could see again. There was little to focus on, except the rear of the thin shambling figure as it hurried on to the next bend, lurching as it went. In a second or two it was out of sight and earshot. The only sound was the beating of rain on the bitumen and the hammering inside her own ears.

Blankly she brought her wrist up to her face. A razor-slash, she had heard, could be painless for a moment, insidious in its lethal effect. She could see nothing. A pool seemed to be forming at her feet: in a panic she leapt aside, peered at the ground and saw only transparent wetness. Trembling she dabbed at herself. She was soaked through but she seemed to be intact.

Her knees gave way. Half-falling, she grabbed and held on to the railings, staying there until she had regained control of her muscles. When she pushed herself clear, she found it impossible to avoid swaying as if she had been on the booze.

Part of her wanted to go on, to eliminate the gap between herself and carpeted floors and hot radiators and lively chatter. Another part was trying to veto the venture. Ahead lay the bend: beyond it, danger might still lurk. Retreating to the street would achieve...what? She had to move. She was drenched, chilled through and, for heaven's sake, two minutes from home; one healthy shriek would bring somebody running. But why shriek? You could attract the wrong attention that way.

Left foot first. Then the right. After two or three false starts she rediscovered the rhythm. Her shoes squelched. Keep going. She had no choice. It was forward or back, and she wasn't going back, not now, not for anything; that hot bath was waiting, calling to her. She kept her thoughts on heated water gushing from chromium taps, the caress of scented soap. Mum would be striding about the kitchen, slamming dishes into oven and sink. *How'd you make out, love? All right, except for that Sheila creature*. By now, Sheila would be indoors. Clumping around, shaking the house. Imagine anyone trying to attack *her* in a dark alley...

Julie's stomach seemed to collapse.

She was past the bend and there he was, ahead of her, waiting. She didn't pull up. She kept walking, because it was one degree better than coming to a halt and standing like a hypnotized rabbit; she continued the progression of one foot before the other in defiance of the forces screaming at her to stop. And as the distance shrank, she realized with an inner sob of relief that instinct had got it wrong. It wasn't the lean, loping figure, emitting gasps. This one was solid, upright and female, sheltering beneath an umbrella and looking lost. At Julie's approach, it turned.

'I'm looking for Lewis House.'

The voice, quaintly in a woman of such majesty, verged on the falsetto. Julie felt an uncontrollable urge to giggle. 'It's over there,' she said, disguising the impulse by turning to point. 'Which number flat did you want?'

'Eighty-three.'

'They don't go up to eighty-three.' It was marvellous to talk normally, on a matter of such banality.

'Perhaps I've got it wrong.' Lowering the umbrella, the woman opened her shoulder-sling bag. Julie waited for her to produce a slip of paper. The bag, she guessed, was like her own, so stuffed with junk that the things one wanted were always at the bottom. The woman's hand emerged with something, but it wasn't paper.

'Try again,' prompted Julie. 'It's there somewhere.'

'No,' the woman said politely. 'This will do perfectly well.'

Julie's last thought, just before the cord went around her neck, was that the falsetto voice had become much deeper.

CHAPTER 8

Melvyn Deans signalled to his deputy on the News Desk.

'We could have something here.'

Alan Cranshaw studied the postcard. Turning it over, he squinted at the marked side before reversing it again and re-reading the message. 'This come through the post? No stamp.'

Deans held up a plain, buff envelope.

'Better take your sticky fingers off it,' Cranshaw advised.

Together, they examined the stationery.

'Block capitals,' murmured Deans. 'Fibre-tip pen.'

'Neat characters.'

'Somebody with a tidy mind.'

'Or mindless.'

'I don't know about that,' Deans said thoughtfully. 'He seems literate.'

'Reckon we should take it seriously?'

The News Editor reached a decision.

'Get 'em both photographed. Then we'll inform the law.'

Later editions of the *Echo* that afternoon carried frontpage reproductions of the two postal items. The envelope was addressed to THE CRIME EDITOR, EVENING ECHO, LONDON, EC4. The postcard's message, meticulously spaced, in black ink, was confined to one side.

THE NEXT BLAST WILL BE SOMETHING. ANY GUESSES? DATE, TIME, SITUATION? HAVE A TRY. IT ADDS TO THE PIQUANCY. NOT LONG TO GO NOW, SO BE QUICK. NEMESIS.

The originals, the *Echo* announced piously, had been handed to the police for forensic analysis. The card in its envelope had arrived by second delivery under a first-class stamp with a London postmark.

The reason it was being taken seriously by Special Branch, the report went on, was its similarity to a previous message sent to the head office of a weekly newspaper in Fulham, shortly before the first bomb explosion at the Grill Room in South Kensington. This had immediately been passed to the authorities, who had asked the publication concerned to stay quiet about the matter.

After the second blast, however, in which more than forty youngsters at the Blue Spark Disco in Wood Green had been slaughtered, the editor had broken silence, forcing official confirmation that 'an anonymous communication' had in fact been received before the atrocities started. In no way had it assisted the police in preventing either catastrophe.

'Any more than this one promises to,' remarked Alan Cranshaw in the Press Club bar.

'They reckon it's from the same nut?' The question was put in an idle manner by the chief crime reporter of the *Enquirer*, who had no real expectation of a constructive answer and was neither surprised nor perturbed when Cranshaw replied, 'Scratch your own sources, old boy, and leave ours to us.'

Somebody else said, 'It's only the

bloody Irish.'

'I don't know about that,' said the *Enquirer* man, meditating over his beer.

'Neither do I,' agreed Cranshaw unexpectedly, eliminating a double Scotch. 'This one's in a new dimension, if you ask me.'

Miss Manning had moved the table six inches closer to the window.

Either she had wanted to spread the wear on the carpet or she had been searching for something. Without troubling to move it back he opened the cupboard door and restocked the interior with a few essentials he had brought in: instant coffee, molasses sugar, long-life milk, a packet of rich tea biscuits. When everything was packed away, he folded the carrier bag into a pocket of his coat and smacked it flat before stepping across to the mirror for a final check. Then he let himself out of the room.

For a moment he hesitated on the landing. Finally, with a shrug, he relocked the door, pocketed the key and went downstairs.

The driver of the hired car was a garrulous Midlander. 'Beefing about snow, they are. You'd think the stuff'd just been invented. Frightens 'em, it does. X the Unknown. Got 'em all arse ends up. It's not even arrived yet. They want something to be scared about, they should concentrate on bomb maniacs. Them I do find hairy, I'm telling you. Reckon they'll trace this freak?'

After a gear-changing pause, the driver added pensively, 'Speaking personally, I don't see as how anyone can get a line on a nutter like this. Not unless he's daft enough to give himself away. What's to stop him just carrying on, stooling around, enjoying his bleeding self?'

Alison came to the door. She was wearing a heavy green and tangerine sweater above a black skirt of mid-calf length, hemmed with a white material that danced as she moved. Her hair was drawn back, accentuating the high curves of her cheeks and seeming to enlarge her eyes. She had coloured her lips more vividly than usual. 'Hi,' she said.

'Hi.'

'What time does the big film start?'

'Eight-twenty.'

'Time for you to come in, then, and meet Mother. If you'd like to.'

'Sure.'

The hall was well carpeted, but cold. Closing the door, Alison turned and looked at him seriously.

'Had something to eat? You're certain? I can easily...' Breaking off, she advanced and put her arms about his waist, pressed her face against his chest. 'Hi,' she repeated.

Her shoulders were firm under his touch. The scent of her hair merged with that of the sweater to form a subtle blend. They stood in silence until he straightened his arms, moving her away to a position from which she gazed slightly to one side of him, like someone trying to view the sun. When he took his hands away, she gave a small shake of the head as if emerging from sleep.

'Your mother?' he asked.

She took his hand. 'Come through.'

Leading him to the back of the house, she propelled him into a long, split-level living room, curtained the entire length of one side. At the far end of the sunken half a blonde-headed woman sat in a curved leather-upholstered chair with a steel frame on castors, her calves supported by a matching footstool. She was reading a paperback. In contrast to the hall, the room shimmered with heat from vents in the skirting. At their approach, she looked up.

Alison said, 'This is Colin.'

'I never imagined it was the tax inspector, my love.' A languid arm snaked towards him. 'Leading my daughter astray, are you, sinful man? Intriguing to meet you. Do sit down, I shall get a crick in the neck. You're not as Alison described you. Not the *tiniest* bit.'

'I don't remember trying to describe him.'

'Exactly. You weren't *trying*. Anyway it doesn't matter now, I can see for myself. Well, you were right about the hair, at least.' Her own was darker at the roots than elsewhere; hanging straight at the sides, it was finished in a fringe across the temples, squaring off a face that would otherwise have displayed a Sitwellian superabundance of forehead and jawline. Perfume gusted from her. 'The hair and the eyes. He certainly *looks* artistic. You're a sculptor, my daughter tells me.'

'I said he could be. Don't embarrass him. Fancy a drink, Colin? We've got whisky or—'

'A drinkie, what a divine idea. Bring the bottle, darling, and some goblets. Now, Colin. I'm not going to ask you all about yourself, because I can see you're one of these deep mysterious beings who prefer to hug it to themselves, and goodness me why not?' A trousered knee crossed its twin in an elegant swoop. 'Of course, assuming that you *were* something in the creative line, I might possibly be of some... Did my forgetful daughter chance to tell you? I'm with a firm of auctioneers and valuers. Ambere's. You may have heard of us.'

'Best in the business.'

'We do try. A household name...well, no, unlike one or two I could mention. But candidly, my dear, we have a better reputation in the trade and that counts for a lot, believe you me. Now, in the hypothetical event that you were in the market...'

'You're not pitching Colin the spiel already?'

'What does it sound like, my pet? I don't think he's listening, though. I don't believe he's taking the *slightest* notice.'

'When he looks like that he's listening intently.'

'You'd know, of course. Give Colin a very large Glenlivet with a very small splash. Not driving, are you, Colin? I gather you hire your vehicles, complete with pilot...very grand. The last friend Alison brought home—'

'All right, Mother, we needn't go into all that.'

'I was only going to tell Colin about the motor-bike.'

'He's heard.'

'You spoil all my best stories.' Alison's mother pouted, surveying him sidelong. 'Talking of narrative, do you mind if I switch on to Channel Nine at seven-thirty? Frightfully antisocial of me I know, but it's episode three of that rather riveting new thriller, *Knife Edge*, and once I lose the thread—'

'You don't have to worry, we're off to

the cinema. You can have the set to yourself.' Alison distributed glasses. After a fastidious sip, her mother placed it aside.

'What are you seeing?'

'Threesome.'

The pointed nose of the older woman wrinkled in distaste. 'Your idea, poppet, I don't doubt.'

'Of course it was,' Alison said cheerfully.

'I'm sure Colin must view the prospect with nausea.'

'I gave him a choice. He said he didn't mind where we went, so long as I served him with his nails.'

Mrs Duke turned slowly in her chair to fix a prolonged survey upon her daughter.

'I expect it's the whisky,' she said, on a faint note, 'but I could have sworn you said something about *nails*.'

'That's right. Colin buys no end of them.'

'Is one permitted to ask...for what purpose?'

'He won't say.' Alison leaned against the arm of a chair. 'My guess is, he uses them for some advanced form of sculpture.'

Her mother turned back. 'And you deny it?'

'I don't use them for knocking into fences.'

'Now that's what I call a *very* cagey answer. *Highly* enigmatic. I shall worry about this all night. *Nails*. My precious child, what have you done to your jaded parent? You've brought a conundrum into the house.'

'No need to agonize about it,' Alison advised. 'I don't.'

'That's easy to say. You just sell the things. To someone with imagination... I've got it,' she announced, moulding one side of her hair with a graceful palm. 'Toy soldiers! You melt them down to make—no, that can't be right. Who ever heard of two-inch nails made of lead?'

'He buys three-inch.'

'Then I'm at a loss. Leave me,' she commanded, settling back in a flounce of trousered buttock, 'to study my *Knife Edge* and ponder the problem. Are you going to be late?'

'Probably not,' Alison said with a quick glance.

'Well, whatever time it is, creep in

quietly, there's a lamb. I've an important client to see tomorrow. He wants us to auction his collection of Spode. So *nice* to meet you, Colin. How cold your hand is. You've ruined my peace of mind, but I forgive you. One day you *will* tell us, won't you, what you do with your three-inch nails? That's a dear boy. I suppose I should call you that, though truly I think that you and I are closer to being contemporaries, in fact it occurs to me... However. Have a *marvellous* time, the pair of you, and shut the door on your way out.'

Whimpering under the brake the car nudged the kerbstone with a rubber elbow. The driver cut the engine.

The outline of the building could dimly be seen. Alison peeped out at the upper windows. 'Which one is yours?'

'Right at the top. Take a look inside?'

'Okay.'

As they entered the hall and embarked on the stairs, she said, 'You didn't enjoy the film, did you?'

'I enjoyed the evening.'

Between Miss Manning's door and its

frame, a crack appeared and widened. It remained until they were out of sight, and then was stealthily extinguished.

'It's a good way up,' said Alison, breathlessly, on the third landing.

'Away from traffic noise.' Unlocking the door, he switched on the light. The curtains were already drawn. She stood looking silently around the room. Closing the door, he turned on the electric fire and went across to the cupboard. 'Coffee?'

'Mmm, please.'

She observed his preparations. A second cup from the cupboard joined the existing one on top. Filling the kettle and switching it on, he wrenched open a carton of sterilized milk. She nodded towards it.

'Handy stuff, that.'

'Sit yourself somewhere.'

As she had done in her own house, she perched on an arm of the solitary chair. When the coffee was made he handed her a cup and stood nearby, clasping the other with both hands, staring at the cold fireplace as he drank. Her own gaze she divided between the tiles and his face.

'You just have the one room?' she asked.

'Just the one. There's a bathroom on the floor below.'

'You must feel cooped up sometimes.'

'I'm out a lot.'

'Buying nails?'

'Or using them.'

She stretched across to place her cup on the table. 'Mother will have a theory about your nails by the morning.'

'I daresay.'

'What did you think of her?'

'She looks young.'

'She had me when she was eighteen. That makes her forty. Wears well, doesn't she?'

'I never saw her when she was younger.'

'She's probably regretting that.'

Below, in the street, a wavelet of traffic rippled past, creating a foam of noise in the night. In its wake, the intermittent purr of a telephone bell could faintly be heard. Presently it stopped. There was no sound except for the hint of a rattle from the shrouded window, a hum from the electric fire.

'Look, there's something I want to explain. I knew she'd behave like that, the instant she set eyes on you. She always does. I haven't minded, other times. It hasn't meant that much to me.'

'It's not important.'

'I suppose it isn't. It's just that I'd rather like to know where I stand. I'm not being bitchy about it. Trying hard not to be. I know I must seem young to you...'

'Your chair's tipping up.'

She adjusted her weight so that the chair returned to the floor with a thump. Smiling, she said, 'That's wrecked their beauty sleep below. I hope you don't think I'm naïve, bringing this up so soon. It's partly the reason I wanted you to come home and meet her. The main reason, actually. To get it over with. See how you reacted.'

'And how did I react?'

'I couldn't make out. I know how *she* reacted. By now I'm familiar with the ritual: I ought to be. What effect it had on you... This is why I was asking.'

'I see.'

'I've no right to put the question. It's

not as if I had any claim over you at all. But quite honestly I can't help myself. Sorry if I've...messed things up between us. Lack of confidence, I suppose. She hasn't left me with much.'

'You seem to cope with her quite well.'

'It's all surface noise. You probably don't hear the undertones. Behind the brittle chat there's a war going on. And I can't shake myself of the idea that she's winning.'

'It takes two to make a war.'

Alison looked at the table. After a moment she said, 'You can have a darn good fight with yourself sometimes.'

She stood up, fumbling with her coat buttons, letting her gaze roam. 'I can see you could be quite snug up here. Left to yourself, too, I should think. No one to interfere. Gets nice and warm, doesn't it, when the fire's been on a bit. The bed looks comfy.'

She went over and stood looking down at its lumps. When she turned, her coat loosened, there was a brightness in her eyes. At his approach, she took a quick audible breath and parted her lips, staring up at him like a novitiate at a pagan rite. Her arms became slack. In response to his touch, her body gave a small jump and then was motionless, rigid in expectancy.

'Time to go,' he said, leading her to the door. 'Your mother will be worried about you.'

CHAPTER 9

'Sit down, gentlemen,' said the Chief.

Cullen and Royce took the available chairs. The other three were occupied already by men of divergent personalities. One of them was balding and hollow-cheeked, with a neck at an anxious angle to his shoulders; another was plump and self-possessed, in his mid-forties. The third, a straight-backed individual of about fifty, epitomized the popular image of an examining magistrate.

The Chief flipped a thick hand. 'Chief Inspector Cullen and Inspector Royce of the Squad. Chief Super Bellamy you're acquainted with, I believe, both of you, from happier days.'

They grinned and nodded. The plump man gave them a genial smile. The Chief went on, 'The same can't be said, I know, of Commander Asherton of C Department. The Commander, as you know, is in overall charge of operations in connection with this current spot of bother.'

The magisterial Asherton bent an attentive look upon the two Squad men. 'How are things going?'

Royce said, 'I'm afraid, sir, we're not getting very far.'

'And finally,' added the Chief inexorably, 'I'd like you to meet our Mr Somerfield of the Police Laboratory.'

The balding man rose and shook hands punctiliously, the angle between his neck and shoulders increasing to a disturbing degree. Waiting patiently until he had resumed his seat, the Chief ignited a small cigar and, through the fumes, said to Commander Asherton, 'Care to take it from here?'

'We're having this minor conference,' the Commander explained to Cullen and Royce, 'in an attempt to avoid any slip-ups resulting from lack of liaison. As you're aware, basically the problem seemed to be one for the Squad, which does a grand job, a thankless job...'

He and the Chief exchanged inclinations of the head. 'However, as far as we can make out, a new dimension has crept into this one. All enquiries so far seem to indicate that none of the established groups is involved. Much as they'd like to be, no doubt. But in these enlightened times,' the Commander added sardonically, 'those aiming at political targets apparently feel obliged to keep at least half an eye on their world image. Agreed?'

Cullen nodded again. 'Quite often there's a warning, at least.'

'Or some element of selectivity?'

After some hesitation Cullen said, 'I'd go along with that.'

Royce stirred. 'This is largely what's been holding us up.'

'Carry on, Inspector.'

'Well sir, to my way of thinking, something as indiscriminate as this calls for a new approach. Take the Squad. We've all been flogging along well-worn tracks, talking to the usual crowd, hoping for a lead from someone who doesn't much care for what's been happening. We've got nowhere. Which seems significant to me. It suggests that what you were saying just now is right—none of the known groupings is responsible.'

'That's how it strikes me,' said Cullen.

The Commander studied them. 'You mentioned a fresh approach...'

Royce glanced at the Chief. 'If our surmise stands up, haven't we got to broaden the whole scope of the investigation? To include, possibly, anyone with a record of psychopathic behaviour plus a working knowledge of explosives. It's a tall order, but do we have an alternative?'

'No,' said Asherton, 'we don't. Hence this meeting. You've made a valid point, Inspector. It's certainly on the cards that what we're faced with here is a one-man blitz motivated by some mental disorder. The complications—'

'Can I ask a question, sir?' asked Cullen.

'Go ahead.'

'This girl, Julie Morris, who was found strangled yesterday. Has it been decided whether her killing was coincidental, or if there's a connection?'

'Let's just say, the likelihood is being kept strongly in mind.'

A movement came from Chief Superintendent Bellamy. 'It's not strictly my field, but having regard to the circumstances I'd lay high odds on a link.'

The Chief tapped away ash. 'I agree.'

Asherton said, 'Just one other possibility occurs to me...'

'What's that, sir?'

'That someone in or around Wood Green has homicidal tendencies anyway, and that when he read about Julie Morris in the Press his imagination was excited. Pretty teenage survivor of bomb blast, and so forth. Her home address was published, don't forget. It shouldn't have been, but it was. Perhaps that was all it needed to spur a would-be strangler into making plans.'

'It's a theory,' Bellamy conceded thoughtfully.

'But a pale one by comparison.' The Chief's candour drew a quizzical look from Asherton. 'Granted, there are screwballs around whose fantasies feed on the things they hear and read about—but plenty of other girls from that area must have got themselves into the news lately. Why Julie? Julie was special, that's why. Bob?'

Royce sat forward. 'Shortly after the disco bombing I interviewed Julie. She was able to tell me a fair bit about the man she spoke to. In view of this, I did consider round-the-clock protection for her, but the risk seemed rather remote and I decided that a word of caution—'

'Bob discussed it with me,' Cullen interposed, 'and I agreed with him that protection didn't seem called for. With hindsight, that was a wrong decision.'

'But understandable,' said the Chief. 'We've a manpower problem.'

Asherton made no comment.

'Had we done as we originally intended,' added Cullen, 'Julie would have had Sergeant Ferguson keeping an eye on her...and there might have been a very different outcome to the story. Not only would Julie have been alive now, but we might have—'

'Yes, well, Chief Inspector, there's no point in agonizing over it. You did as you thought best.'

'Not quite true, sir. I had doubts. But a promising line of enquiry opened up in the Paddington area, and it seemed more productive for Ferguson to look into that than to spend nights as a watchdog. So I took what seemed an acceptable chance and let him get on with it.'

'And nothing's come from that, I suppose?'

'Ferguson seems hopeful. Apparently it's some Irish character, not known to us, who's been shooting his mouth off in the clubs. Ferguson's staying close to him. Trying to get his confidence.'

'Well, that sounds a little auspicious.'

'We're not setting too much store by it, sir. Ferguson's had these enthusiasms before. Occasionally they've led to something, so it's probably worthwhile giving him his head for a few days. That's as far as I'd go.'

The Commander grunted.

'Getting back to the question of protection,' said Bellamy, with some diffidence, 'what about this other girl...the Grill Room survivor?'

'Still in hospital,' Cullen told him. 'We've a man outside her door, day and night.'

Bellamy's plump face went into folds. 'And when she's discharged? We can't guard her for ever. If despite our best efforts the bomber remains at large...'

Cullen coughed. 'An idea,' he said reluctantly, 'has been mooted. The suggestion is that we might use her as a decoy.'

Asherton puffed his cheeks. 'Chancy. Don't care for it.'

Bellamy fashioned some grimaces of his own. 'The set-up would need to be foolproof. Besides, would the bomber feel inclined to press his luck again? He scored with Julie Morris, if what we're assuming is right. But then, she perhaps represented rather more of a threat. Or he thought she did. I don't know.'

'Who had this idea?' asked the Commander.

'Ferguson, sir. As I say, his thinking tends to be a bit wild at times, but this was a notion I thought should at least be passed on.'

Asherton glanced at the Chief, whose scrutiny swung towards Royce. 'What do you say, Bob?'

Royce sat silently for several moments before speaking. 'She's got guts. If any girl could handle it, I reckon she could.'

'It would have to be a very last resort.'

'On the other hand, of course,' murmured the Chief, 'we do have a situation in which somebody is writing in block capitals to the Press, bragging of an imminent disaster. It could be a hoax. Last time, though, it wasn't, apparently.'

Asherton said, 'I'm aware of the pressures.'

'What's the state of the enquiries into Julie's death?'

'Not promising. Apart from a girlfriend of hers, who last saw her setting out to walk home from the station, nobody seems to have noticed her except a lad of fifteen who says he passed her on the footpath leading to the flats. That must have been very shortly before she was attacked. The heavy rain—'

'A lad of fifteen,' Bellamy repeated.

Asherton regarded him dourly. 'No use getting ideas. We've eliminated the boy.'

'How come?'

'He's got a spinal deformity which means he can't use his hands. Whatever else the killer may lack, it's not strength of finger. Right, Somerfield?'

The balding man hastened to concur.

'The fellow we're after,' he added, with a trace of a Suffolk dialect, 'is distinctly vigorous in that department.'

'I thought the girl was garotted,' said the Chief.

'A cord of some kind was used,' Somerfield confirmed. 'But even the use of that would have taken a certain vigour and dexterity.'

'Which the boy simply doesn't possess,' said Asherton. 'It's questionable, anyhow, whether he could have got himself into a position to attack Julie in the first place. He's smaller than she was.'

Bellamy grunted.

'What's more, he was the first to come forward with information.'

'What does that prove?'

'Nothing. But in view of the lad's disability,' observed the Chief, 'we can obviously rule him out. I take it he doesn't recall seeing anyone else around at the time?'

Asherton said, 'I was about to mention, the heavy rain had driven everyone off the streets. According to the boy—his name's Nigel Turner—the footpath was deserted apart from himself and the girl.'

'But she was only a couple of hundred yards from home,' objected Royce. 'How fast was this Nigel walking?'

'He says he was hurrying, though apparently he can't work up much of a pace. But he also says the girl pulled up as he passed her, as if she was out of breath. She may have stood there a while.'

'In pelting rain, sir?'

The Commander lifted both hands. 'It's supposition, I grant. But she could have had her own reasons for wanting Nigel to get ahead. He's...poor young man, he's not frankly the most edifying of sights. He has facial peculiarities, into the bargain.'

'Bloody unfair,' Bellamy said softly.

'Right, Clive. Same old unjust world. The one where murderers can nip in, do the job and nip out again without being seen by a mortal soul.'

'There ought to be a law against it,' the Chief said drily.

'And another, banning the right of psychopaths to exist. Unhappily, you'd have an enforcement problem. First spot your lunatic.'

'I'd make a start at Westminster,' growled the Chief.

'Returning to the matter in hand,' said Asherton, shifting his chair so that Somerfield was brought into greater prominence, 'we've a lab report, I believe, on the explosive devices used at the Grill Room and disco?'

The hollow-cheeked laboratory man carried out a nervous clearing of the throat and consulted some notes. 'It's necessarily somewhat speculative. From tests carried out on the impactive force—'

'Keep it simple, Roy.'

'Very good, sir. From the distribution of the nails, depths to which they were embedded in walls, et cetera, we've estimated an explosive content of something in the order of a pound or possibly two pounds of material...'

'In each case?'

'Quite so. For a device of this nature, it's not essential to incorporate a great weight of jelly. The nails in a confined space are what cause the damage.'

'Type of nail?'

'Ordinary three-inch wire. The kind

you can buy from practically any hardware store.'

'Nothing special about them?'

'Only that for maximum effect the heads had been filed to a point.'

'Delightful. We have a dedicated craftsman to contend with, it seems. Presumably it wouldn't be too difficult for someone with the technical know-how to run up a neat little package like this in his shed or garage?'

'No trouble whatever,' Somerfield agreed. 'He could do it on his kitchen table.'

'How about the timing mechanism?'

'An alarm watch could be used. A high degree of accuracy could be achieved, as evidently it was. The entire thing could be packed into relatively few cubic inches.'

'At the disco,' remarked the Chief, 'it was mistaken by Julie Morris for a bundle of newspapers.'

Asherton rubbed his jaw. 'Question is, how many people—individuals—might be expected to have the aptitude to assemble one of these things successfully ...twice running?'

'Bob? You're the expert.'

With a glance at Cullen, Royce said, 'What area are we talking about? London, or the country as a whole? Either way, there's virtually no limit to the number of gifted amateurs capable of doing something in that line if they like to read up about it.'

Somerfield nodded assent. 'Of course, they've got to get hold of the explosive.'

'That does narrow the field. But it still leaves acres of open space. In London alone, during the last wave of political bombings, with the aid of sniffer dogs we turned up—what, a couple of dozen separate caches, Harry? In back rooms, cellars, attics...all over the shop. And they were probably just the tip of the ice berg. I don't think anyone with enough motivation need go short of a supply source.'

The Commander looked discouraged. He said to Cullen, 'How about the latest blitz?'

'We've pulled in a few regulars. They've all had brick-hard alibis for the nights in question.'

Asherton looked around the group.

'The feeling I'm getting,' he said deliberately, 'is that we don't hold many trumps at the moment.'

'Except possibly one,' said Bellamy. 'And she's on her back in bed.'

CHAPTER 10

'Not that there's any rush,' Miss Manning averred. 'Next time you see me will do.'

'I'd sooner you took it now.'

'You'd better come inside, then, while I enter it in the book.' She held the door for him. 'I'm just cooking my bit of supper.'

Of this there was substantial confirmation, of a nature both olfactory and auditory, from the region of the immense kitchen which formed part of Miss Manning's ground-floor labyrinth. Onion predominated. Delicately closing the kitchen door, she led the way through to a cavernous lounge infested with furniture and pulsing with heat. At one end of the room a gas fire of cathedral-organ dimensions was producing radiation on the scale of a small nuclear reactor; at the other, an electric device sheathed in steel and chrome was discharging baked air with a sustained hiss. Flattening the rent book across the uncovered portion of a gate-leg table, she began scratching at it with a ballpen she had removed in passing from an empty vase on a side-board.

'Not leaving us, Mr Wood, are you?'

'I've no plans to.'

'Only I thought I saw you bring some-one back the other night. And it did strike me, you might be showing them the accommodation with a view to—'

'It was a friend of mine.'

'Oh, I see.' Miss Manning wrote busily. 'Just a friend. I thought possibly it might be that, only she didn't seem to stop long and that's what made me wonder. Just a social call.' She breathed noisily upon the ink. 'Interested to see where you lived, she was, I expect. I do like people to feel they can bring their friends back. Always providing there's no noise, we can't have the other resi-dents disturbed, but so long as there's a responsible attitude on the part of all concerned...'

Closing the rent book, she handed it to him while folding the banknotes deftly into a heavy mahogany box, the lid of which she then allowed to drop with a thud and the sound of meshing metallic parts. 'Pleased to hear you're not thinking of pulling your roots up, not yet awhile at all events. I was saying the other day to my friend Mrs Townsend, she's in charge of a block just along the street, I'm lucky, I said, in the people I've with me at the moment, particularly the gentleman on the attic floor, I said. Unless you're careful, I said, you can find yourself stuck with someone that puts on heavy boots every time he crosses the floor, or shifts the furnishings around every other minute. I've had experience, I can tell you. Never a hint of anything like that from you, Mr Wood, I'm glad to say.'

'Thank you.' He pocketed the rent book.

'And I do like to hear a bit of music. Providing there's no complaint from the other residents, I don't mind how loud people have their radios on, within reason of course. There's reason in all things, isn't there? That's what I always say. My friend Mrs Townsend—'

'Does my music disturb anyone?'

'Oh, I'm quite sure it doesn't. Mind you, they might not necessarily say, if you know what I mean. They might not like to.'

'It's up to them.'

'Of course it is. To my mind, a spot of classical music never did anyone a bit of harm. Fond of your classics, aren't you, Mr Wood? You don't belong to one of these record societies, by any chance? I wondered. I thought perhaps your friend the other night had come back to hear a new recording. But of course, there wouldn't have been time. I just happened to be putting the empty milk bottles out when she—'

'I must be off.'

'Out on business?' she asked, eyeing his briefcase. 'Or amusing yourself for the evening?'

'Something of each. Good night, Miss Manning.'

After the room, the street was a ventilated vault under the arched ceiling of the night sky. Turning left, he walked to the junction and joined a queue of three at the bus stop. Boarding the second bus that came along, he bought the lowest-priced ticket and occupied a seat near the folding doors, the briefcase clasped squarely across his knees.

At the third stop he dismounted. Nobody else left or entered the bus. When it had groaned away into the gloom he turned and walked into a side street flanked on both sides by derelict property, twin ramparts of rotting brick and stucco and twisted railings, dimly lit by sodium lamps on old-fashioned wrought columns. Corrugated iron, autumn-tinted, covered doors and windows. Crossing the road, he continued to a point where the ramshackle facade expired with its nose to a tall fence of chain-link that bore a printed notice: GREATER LONDON COUNCIL SITE FOR 280 DWELLINGS.

At the base of the fence in a corner a section of the linkage had been unravelled and dragged back. With a swift rearward glance he ducked through the gap and followed a track between piles of weed-festooned rubble, past the end of the building to what had once been a triangular garden at the back. Remnants of stakes and wire netting marked forgotten boundaries. Treading through the nettles he reached a flight of stone steps that ascended to an oblong opening, devoid of door.

Here the darkness was almost total. From a pocket of his coat he produced a small torch which he shone through the entrance. The beam showed a floor of decaying linoleum over boards. A stench of mildew hung in the air.

He stepped through, committing his weight with caution. Holes gaped between eaten joists. Mouldering plaster lay in heaps. A dozen watchful paces took him to the wreck of an inner room, where traces of a dark-hued wallpaper were discernible in the midst of expanses of lath and plaster.

Shading the torch he picked his way across to the tiled hearth that occupied the centre of a wall, knelt, placed the briefcase gently aside with the torch on top of it, leaned forward, and inserted an arm into the chimney space.

After a moment's fumbling he withdrew the arm, bringing with it a polythene-wrapped bundle which he deposited on the hearth and commenced to unravel.

An assortment of clothing emerged. Windcheaters, a jacket, scarves, sweaters. Three pairs of shoes, one of them a woman's with platform heels. There was also a woman's coat with fur-trimmed collar.

Removing the coat and shoes he was wearing he studied the selection. Presently he picked out a high-necked sweater and the jacket, and a pair of casual shoes in pigskin. Opening a smaller parcel from the centre of the bundle he spread out the wigs and false moustaches it contained, and meditated over them for a while. Having made his choice he changed swiftly.

The clothing and other items he had removed went into the polythene bag, and the bundle was restored to its recess inside the chimney. The operation had taken nine minutes.

Picking up torch and briefcase he returned with the same care to the rear entrance, where he killed the light before making his way back to the gap in the fence.

The street lay in utter silence. Walking easily, unhurriedly back to the junction with the main road, he crossed over and continued another two hundred yards to the Tube station.

* * * *

From Leicester Square he strolled through a street or two of sex shops and Chinese restaurants into Shaftesbury Avenue.

The foyer of the King's Theatre was filled to capacity and beyond. People spilled from the front doors and over the pavement. Attaching himself to the fringe, he stood waiting, studying the framed clippings of Press reviews as the queue inched forward.

'A Memorable Evening.'

'Pure magic as Corbison weaves his spell...'

'Box Office Blockbuster!'

Behind him a girl said to her companion, 'It always seems to me the newspaper critics have seen a different play from the one I get tickets for.'

A breeze whipped the street.

'Adrian Halifax, one of the finest of our younger generation of theatrical performers...'

Inside the foyer, handbags and other belongings were being inspected by a trio of theatre staff. Progress was snail's-pace. The girl said, 'I know it's a good idea and it has to be done, but I wish they'd hurry it up. We'll miss the first act at this rate.'

The tallest of the examiners said, 'If I could just see your briefcase, sir.'

Releasing the clasps, he held it out, having first extracted a pound box of chocolates which he showed to the man with a smile. 'I take it these will be allowed inside with me? They're only injected with cyanide.'

The man glanced at the box. The cellophane seal protected a picture of red roses. Probing the interior of the briefcase with his left hand, he said gravely, 'If your digestion will stand it, sir, I'm sure ours will.' He handed back the briefcase. 'Thank you, sir. Dress circle to your right. Your bag, please, madam...'

At the top of the carpeted staircase an attendant peered at his ticket and directed him to seat 19, row F.

He sat relaxed with his jacket unbuttoned, the briefcase under the seat, the chocolate box on his lap. A middle-aged pair squeezed past him and occupied the next seats. To his left, a female quartet was already established. All of them were munching candies while conning programmes.

Directly in front of him a wild-haired youth in a chunky sweater was in earnest conversation with a thin-faced girl wearing about her neck a heavy silver chain as though she were waiting to be led off. In the centre block of the circle only a handful of seats remained vacant.

Nearby, a woman's Roedean voice said, 'Act One is the *tour de force*, Ronnie says. After that it sags, apparently.'

He sat motionless, hands folded over the chocolate box.

The house lights dimmed.

Exactly forty-two minutes later the second scene of the first act concluded with a piercing scream from the heroine and a buzz from the audience as the curtain fell. Retrieving the briefcase, he rose, leaving the untouched chocolate box on the upturned edge of his seat. With an apology he eased his way past a number of female knees to the gangway, joining the drift to the ice-cream salesgirl and the bar. By-passing the latter, he continued to the unmanned exit, and, without haste, descended the stairs to the foyer. Pausing briefly to examine a poster advertising the next production, he strolled out into the street.

Opposite the theatre was a sandwich bar. He went inside and bought coffee and a slice of gâteau. Seated on a stool at the counter he ate and drank in contemplative manner, his back to the traffic.

Only a couple of other customers were in occupancy. The woman in charge, a square-featured brunette of indeterminate age, had a copy of the *Echo* folded double at her elbow alongside the sandwich container. Between forays for used china, she returned to stare glassily at the crossword clues.

A wall-clock above the counter announced digitally that it was nine-twenty.

Rising once more, the brunette wandered across for his plate. 'Seven letters,' she declared. ' "Come endlessly to one, no matter which, with a soft centre for a firm answer." Make anything of that?'

He thought for a few moments. 'Company.'

'How d'you make that out?'

'A company is a firm.'

'Yah, but...Oh. I get it. "Come endlessly..." That's clever. Devious, that is. Had me sweating for hours, that has.'

'They're meant to relax you.'

'Yah, same as narcotics. Dangerous drugs register, that's where they belong. Here, maybe you can help us out with another one. "Driving force on the links, in partnership with"...' She paused to peer past him through the plate-glass window. 'Somebody been knocked over?'

Unhurriedly he turned to look. A police car, its blue light scintillating, was drawn up outside the King's Theatre. Passers-by had started to congeal into onlookers. As they watched, a second police car arrived in a two-note blare of siren.

'Some poor cuss,' breathed the brunette, 'taken bad inside.'

An elderly female customer who was half-way through a sandwich said sceptically, 'Two squad cars just for that?'

A third appeared. As it snaked to a halt people began to be disseminated from the theatre foyer into the street, where they were escorted by uniformed men to points well clear of the building while traffic was directed around the back of them. The crowd swelled.

'Maybe,' the brunette said, with an uneasy avidity, 'part of the theatre's fallen in. Never did trust them old buildings.' She cupped her mouth. 'Barney! What is it? Accident?'

A young, dwarfish man from the records shop next door looked back over a shoulder. 'Bomb scare,' he said, moodily authoritative.

'You're kidding?'

'Straight up, love. They've called in the disposal squad.'

'Blimey.' The brunette stared nervously from her doorway. 'We okay here?'

A constable approached. 'No panic, Mo. It's right inside the theatre and it's only a little 'un. I'd keep this side, though, if I was you.'

'If you was me,' she retorted, 'you'd be back the other side of that counter, sharpish.' She carried out the manoeuvre. 'Can't stand loud noises,' she confided across the Formica. 'And I don't fancy a faceful of dynamite, either. Hope they've got 'em all out of there. Mind you, it's probably a false alarm. People getting nervous. Nervous! You'd think they'd have more sense.' She cackled a little wildly. 'Here, let's get back to that crossword, take our minds off things. Eleven down, "Driving force on the..." '

'If you'll excuse me,' he said, 'I have to go.'

Quitting his stool, he walked to the doorway where the two other customers had teamed up. 'May I please come through?' Abstractedly they moved aside. Halting on the pavement, he watched over nearby heads as an Army truck drove into the thick of things, pulled up and began to disgorge its cargo of men and equipment. Other traffic in both directions had come to a standstill. He glanced at his watch. It showed nine thirty-seven. He walked off in the direction of Leicester Square.

A rotting floorboard sagged beneath his weight.

Flicking on the torch, he illuminated a narrow band of the ruined kitchen. About to move on, he froze.

From the room beyond had come a sound. The faintest of scuffles, like the brief dart of a rodent.

He remained where he was, looking along the beam towards the connecting doorway.

The sound was not repeated. Presently he resumed his deliberate advance, this time holding the briefcase with greater negligence, letting it swing, not bothering to keep it clear of the doorframe. It connected ringingly. The torchlight swung round, picking out the hearth and chimney-breast, skidding over a dark patch on the floor to the left. Halting once more, he moved the beam around slowly, sweeping the room.

The man looking at him was bearded but not old. He wore a long, shapeless coat over ripped grey trousers with turn-ups, and shoes like canal barges. He stood with his curved spine pressed into a corner, a heap of collapsed plaster at his feet. On the floor beside him stood an immense leather portmanteau of an antiquated design, flaccid and misshapen, its mouth agape: around it were strewn bottles, a half-consumed hamburger on a piece of newsprint, and a number of garments. In his right hand he clutched a wig of dark, wavy hair with a low parting.

The torchlight travelled back to the hearth. The dark patch was the polythene wrapper with its remaining contents arrayed upon it like articles in a jumble sale. Prominent in the display were the other wigs and the shoes, which had been set out in rows. A windcheater, neatly folded, rested alongside.

'I wasn't going to take anything,' said the man from the darkness. 'They were up the chimney. I was just looking.'

'How long have you been here?'

'An hour or so.' The man sounded no more than middle-aged. His speech was clear, touched with a brogue that might have been Irish.

'Why did you come in?'

'I was planning to stop the night. But if I'm intruding in any shape or form...'

'You know perfectly well you're an intruder.'

'From the Council, you'd be?' The man flopped forward, one prow of his footwear catching the half hamburger and knocking it out of range. 'To give you my own personal opinion, I'm doing no harm. But I'm not out for trouble. Show us your authority and I'll be leaving.'

'Are you alone?'

A half-laugh echoed about the walls. 'Aside from me mother and me granny, not to mention the wife and kids and Danny the Donkey, a whole gang of us there are...'

'Get moving.'

'Tell us now, first. What right d'you have to move me on? By what authority?'

'You've thirty seconds.'

The man hesitated. On a sudden decision, he returned to the corner, crouched, stowed his possessions inside the portmanteau. A bottle slipped from his fingers, rolled across the floor towards the door-space.

'Leave it.'

With a shrug, the man picked up the bag by its massive handles in a clinking of glassware, turned and once more came forward, shielding his eyes with a forearm against the torch's glare.

'London's legendary hospitality...' he began.

The bottle had been picked up. Now it swung. As it made contact, the portmanteau flew across the room to strike the farthest wall. In the guiding beam of the torch, the bottle rose and fell twice more. After the third impact, the stillness was total.

CHAPTER 11

'Strict precautions,' said Asherton, 'were supposedly in force at the place. What went wrong?'

The Chief watched the computer stuttering its conclusions endlessly on to paper. 'The human factor,' he explained. 'Someone couldn't rid his mind of the preconception that a chocolate box means all things sweet and nice.'

'Lucky those women in the audience had different ideas.'

'The main stroke of luck...' Lifting the computer sheet, the Chief examined it briefly and let it drop. '...was the failure of the alarm watch inside the package. But for that, they might not have had time to voice their suspicions when the occupant of seat number nineteen failed to return after the interval to claim his soft centres. Next time, things might turn out less happily.'

'There's not to be a next time.'

'That, I take it, is an order?'

Asherton beamed at him. 'You've got it, Reggie. A standing instruction.' He put a hand on the Chief's shoulder. 'You know I'm not one to ask the impossible. We all realize what we're up against. I'm using a figure of speech. At the same time...' His teeth gleamed under the strip lighting. 'I mean it.'

The Chief surveyed the teeth blandly. 'I'll pass your message to the boys.'

'This description we had from the theatre half-wit,' said the Commander, terminating a pause. 'How does it match up with the others?'

The Chief flapped a hand. 'He was tallish, he'd a deepish voice, his dress was nondescript, he didn't stand out in the crowd. The truth is,' added Squad leader, whose vowel-sounds had broadened in rueful mimicry, 'that self-styled analyst of personal belongings was every bit as observant as a senile labrador. "There seemed no reason not to let him through, so I did." Those were his very words to Harry Cullen. A pound box of chocolates...that didn't constitute a reason, oh dear me no.' He kicked the leg of a table.

Asherton seemed disposed to be more tolerant. 'I suppose one has to put oneself in the man's shoes. It was a diabolically clever camouflage, after all. Perfectly done. I might have been fooled myself.'

The Chief's expression left a good deal unsaid. Turning from the computer, he led the way back into the adjoining room where filing cabinets took up much of the available space. Wrenching out one of the drawers, he riffled through it while Asherton inserted a coin in the vending machine beside the door and commenced to thump vainly at buttons.

'White with sugar has packed up,' said the Chief, without looking round. 'You can get black with sugar or white without. No refund.'

'The fallibility of mechanisms,' remarked the Commander on a philosophical note, 'is a mixed drawback. Ask that theatre audience.' Procuring a beaker of black fluid, he sipped at it, winced, stood pondering. 'What do you think,' he asked presently, 'about this morning's Press?'

'You mean, do I regard it as helpful or a kick up the backside?' The Chief shut the drawer with a clash. 'I don't feel it counts for much, either way. Whatever they say or reveal or hint at isn't going to influence this psychopath. Not appreciably. Oh, he might get a lift out of reading about his exploits—the results of them, that is. But he's chosen his path anyway. No, I'm not too bothered about the media. In fact...'

'In fact what?'

'Having regard to the idea advanced by Sergeant Ferguson,' said the Chief, searching his pockets for coinage, 'the Press and TV pundits could finish up making themselves quite useful, for a change.'

'I love it through here,' said Ginny, inhaling deeply.

'As parks go,' Cullen allowed, 'it ranks as one of the less dispiriting variety.'

'Sounds as if you're against them on principle.'

'They've always had a vaguely lowering effect,' he admitted. 'They remind me of damp Sundays. Bible class in the afternoon, followed by a health-giving trek through the recreation ground prior to watercress sandwiches. When I was a lad, Sundays were murder.'

'This afternoon,' she promised, 'you can skip classes.'

'Thanks, teach. How far does this path take us?'

Straight to a teashop at the lakeside. Strictly no watercress.'

'Well, there's a light on the horizon. Ever drag Bob through here, kicking and screaming?'

'Just once. He was pretty good about it. I got him as far as the azaleas: then he remembered he had this appointment with a contact in Pimlico and made his escape by way of the boating pond.'

'Not very brotherly of him.'

'Perhaps it wasn't too sisterly of me to expose him to it. Anyhow we never tried it again. Bob's a city man, he likes the smell of diesel, lots of people around.'

'And you think I'm different?'

'Not necessarily. I was just hoping the incentive might be a little stronger.'

It sounded, she realized instantly,

horribly arch. She wished she had swallowed the remark. For a few yards Cullen walked in silence, apparently lost in thoughts of his own, mental processes which seem to exclude her as firmly as a steel door barring the way to a bank vault. The happiness she had been feeling gave way to despondency. She and her big mouth.

'Maureen and I,' he said suddenly, 'never took a walk together after we were married.'

'I can't believe that.'

'Not,' he insisted, 'in the sense of a *walk*. It wouldn't have occurred to her. There had to be a purpose at the end of it ...buying a bedroom carpet or looting the supermarket.'

She hesitated. 'Maureen sounds like a practical girl.'

Laughter exploded from him. 'That's a typically nice, sincere, Ginny way of expressing it.' He sobered abruptly. 'I shouldn't talk about her. We were two separate people. Probably she found my ways maddening. Who's to blame for what?'

'If anyone knew that,' she said,

'marriage counsellors would barely earn their keep. There's the teashop.'

'You mean that shed with the tin lid and the plastic gnome?'

'Rustic,' she explained. 'Goes with the surroundings.'

'It should have gone some while ago. With or without the surroundings.'

'Wait till you see inside.'

'Okay,' he said, when they were installed. 'It's gnarled, it's quaint, it reeks attractively of dry rot and Rentokil. What do they give you to drink, diluted creosote or the neat stuff?'

'If you're going to be insulting, I'll throw you in the lake.' From the sad-eyed girl who approached them she ordered tea and scones, taking the initiative in a way that Cullen seemed to find entertaining. When the girl had drifted away, they looked at one another across the table.

Cullen said, 'I've spent worse Sunday afternoons.'

'But not many.' She rested her chin on a hand. 'You'd sooner be on duty?'

'Goes without saying.'

'Your flippancy,' she said severely,

'isn't too convincing. I really think you'd like to be getting on with the job, now, this minute.'

'You're right,' he said slowly, 'to the extent that I can never fully relax until I feel that we're getting *somewhere* in an investigation.'

'Which at present you're not?'

His head shook, less in confirmation than uncertainty. Quickly she added, 'Don't let's talk shop. You must feel you want to—'

'We do have one scheme on the stocks,' said Cullen.

She gave him closer attention. He was looking into space. She said tentatively, 'A good one?'

'Has possibilities.' His gaze returned to her. 'It was put up initially by Des Ferguson, and that reminds me of something I wanted to speak to you about. Some while back, Bob mentioned that you'd been considering the idea of taking in a lodger...sorry, fee-paying incumbent. Did you still have it in mind?'

'In a dim sort of way,' she replied, startled. 'It's just that we have this couple of spare rooms upstairs which it seems a pity to waste and I thought, as Bob's out so much... It was just a notion. Why? Is your lease about to expire?'

'Mine isn't,' he said, with what she judged to be a certain haste. 'But you know Des Ferguson's been living permanently at the Rockwood Hotel for the past couple of years? Out of the blue, he's just been told he has to vacate his room in a week's time. They've a rebuilding programme. I think he's going to have problems finding similar accommodation elsewhere, and it occurred to me...'

'I thought he and Bob didn't hit it off too well?'

Cullen smiled. 'It's nothing lethal. Anyhow, the two of them need hardly meet up any more than they do now. And you needn't see much of him, for that matter. He's self-contained. If you gave him a key, he could come and go like a wraith.' He leaned back as their tea arrived. 'I just thought I'd mention it.'

Ginny poured tea for both of them and offered him a scone. Plastering her own with butter, she said uncertainly, 'Really, I'd put the idea out of my head. But if it would help Desmond out of a spot...'

'To be frank,' said Cullen, sipping, 'it would help me.'

'Oh? In what way?'

'It's in connection with this scheme I was talking about just now. If it does go ahead, it could simplify things a lot to have Bob and Desmond under the same roof. And in more general terms, whatever helps to make Squad members happy is a relief to me.'

'If Bob doesn't object, I don't mind. Desmond can come along any time, have a look at the rooms, see what he thinks.'

'Thanks, Ginny. 'You're not saying this just as a favour to me?'

She took a demure mouthful of scone. 'Why would I want to do a thing like that?'

'If it's likely to help,' said Trisha, 'then of course I will.'

Commander Asherton regarded her thoughtfully. 'It might not help in the slightest. We can't predict.'

'Count me in, anyway.'

'And to hell with the risk?'

'Three weeks ago,' she remarked,

touching the bandage about her eyes, 'I'd have said the only possible danger from scoffing smoked salmon in a crowded restaurant was indigestion. Besides, if things worked out, I'd be a heroine, wouldn't I?'

'You are now.'

'Because I managed to survive when a lot of others didn't?'

'That,' said Asherton realistically, 'is Life. The Press has taken you to its bosom. Lovely young model emerges from holocaust...pity you've not been able to read the papers, you'd have been spellbound.'

She snorted. 'When I was a lovely young model, nobody wanted to know. The moment my face is a mess... You have to laugh.'

'In a few months' time,' he told her, 'you'll have regained a pleasing nonentity, along with your looks. If that's any comfort.'

'I'll have to think about it.' After a pause she added, 'Are you fairly tall? About twelve stone, with a lean face and hair brushed back from the temples?'

'Spot-on,' he said, startled. 'How did

you—'

'I'm getting the knack of it.' She heaved herself higher in her chair by the window. 'It's amazing, what you can pick up from a voice. Height's easy, of course. When you said hallo as you came in, I could tell you were taller than average. But the timbre says a lot, too. You sort of pick up the vibes. They announce things like fat! skinny! upright! stooping! They practically draw a picture. You don't believe me?'

'I can hardly do anything else.'

She gurgled. 'Then you're a lousy cop, because I'm having you on. Your Detective-Inspector Royce described you when he was last here: that's how I know.'

He grinned at the bandage. 'You should be on the Force.' He considered her for a moment. 'What else has Inspector Royce been telling you?'

'All about this gambit of yours. Seems an outside chance, to my way of thinking. But I suppose it could work.'

'I've had a word with the surgeon,' said Asherton, perching himself on the windowsill. 'He tells me this eye bandage of yours isn't due off for another couple of days.'

'Right.'

'So what we were tentatively planning was this...'

Trisha listened intently.

Sliding the plate on to the tray across her brother's knees, Ginny sat opposite him and switched on another bar of the electric fire. 'At least,' she said, 'that's one reasonable meal I've managed to force down you this week.'

He nodded absently, absorbed in a late edition of the *Echo*.

'Bob...'

'Uh-huh?'

'I've been thinking about you and Harry. You've both had a good long spell on the Squad. Aren't you about due for desk jobs? Or at any rate something more routine.'

He chopped carefully into the apple pie. 'I really wouldn't know.'

'No one should be asked to keep up this sort of pace indefinitely.'

'Most of the time, we set our own pace.'

'It's a pretty hot one.'

'Well, naturally. We want results.'

'The result in your case could be a breakdown.'

He grinned across at her. 'Do I look to be on the verge?'

Ginny put her own tray aside, the pie untasted. 'I'd sooner you didn't run the risk. I know I've harped on this before, Bob, and I don't want to talk out of turn. But I am your closest surviving relative and I do have the job of looking after you...when you'll let me.'

The grin faded. Relinquishing his fork, he pulled out a pack of cigarettes. 'Sorry, Gin,' he said, lighting one. 'I know I give you a rough deal. I take too much for granted.'

'Of course you do—in respect of yourself, not me. Where's the sense in knocking yourself out?'

He puffed in silence for a while before flicking away ash. 'You know the girl I was telling you about.'

'The one in hospital? The model?'

'Her last bandages are coming off soon.'

'That's good news.' Ginny eyed him obliquely. 'How is she?'

'Facially, you mean? Apparently it could have been a lot worse. They seem to think she'll be fine after some cosmetic surgery.'

'How marvellous. I am glad.' Ginny phrased her question with care. 'Does she have a family to go home to?'

Royce shook his head. 'Her parents split up. She's lost touch with them—thinks they're probably both abroad. She has this bachelor-girl flat in Fulham.'

'And is she going back there?'

'That's the plan.' He drew heavily on the cigarette.

'Is that sensible?'

Scattering more ash, he threw her a glance. 'You don't approve?'

'It's not for me to pass judgments. Do *you* think it's a sound idea?'

He gestured non-committally.

'Whose idea was it, anyway?' she asked. 'Hers? Or was it the outcome of a discussion?' When he said nothing, she added, 'You're going to use her, aren't you? You're hoping she'll lead you to the bomber.'

'She'll have maximum protection. The risk is marginal.'

'Her flat's one of a block, presumably? What if the bomber decided on blanket insurance—blew the entire place sky-high?'

Royce said tolerantly, 'We do take a few of these possibilities into account.'

She meditated for a few moments. 'If it's all cut and dried,' she asked, 'why mention it to me?'

He shrugged. 'You seemed bothered about the pace we were keeping up. I just wanted you to know that there's some chance of a short-cut solution.'

Ginny rose to take his tray. On her knees beside his chair, she gave him an earnest inspection. 'Is that *all* you wanted me to know?'

He looked at her in mild surprise. 'I can't think of anything else, right now.'

Leaving the room, she said across her shoulder, 'As long as none of you is forgetting poor little Julie Morris.'

Her brother picked up the *Echo*. 'We're not forgetting.'

CHAPTER 12

Alison emerged from the back of the shop. Her blue coverall was streaked with dust and there was a smudge on one side of her chin. In her eyes there was uncertainty. 'Hi,' she said. 'Running short of nails again?'

'Anyone else about?'

'Just me at the moment. Mr Free-bottle—'

With a glance towards the shop entrance, he steered her swiftly into the twilight of an unused display recess, crushing her against the chipboard wall. Gasping under his weight, she shut her eyes and clasped her hands behind his neck: when he made a move to release her, she clung on. Below the shop, a boiler activated itself with a thump, feeding pulsations into the flooring. A rack of china cups tinkled faintly.

'Vibro-massage,' she whispered into his ear.

He held her off. 'Where's Freebottle?'

'Popped round to the bank. Where've you *been*? It's four days since—'

'I've had a lot to do.'

'Casting your latest metal masterpiece?'

'You could say that. How's your mother?'

She stiffened. 'Healthy.'

A loud tapping on the display window prompted her to withdraw for a look. Returning, she reclaimed her position. 'Just a horrible small boy with a coin or something. He's gone now.' She leaned back, examining his face. 'Four days is a long time.'

'I've had things on my mind.'

'What things?'

'Trouble with my landlady.'

'Tell me,' she said, her face serious.

'She's been snooping. We had a slight argument, so I've quit.'

'Have you found somewhere else?'

'Just temporary. I'm looking for somewhere more suitable. There's just one problem.'

Standing on tiptoe with her hands resting lightly on his shoulders, she said encouragingly, 'What's the problem?'

'My gear. Some materials and a few tools that need keeping in a safe place. Where I can get at them when I want.'

'Is there much?'

'A couple of suitcases.'

'Why not leave them with me?'

'You don't want to be lumbered.'

'Don't be silly. It's easy. We've got this huge garage at the side of the house that we never use. It's dry and there's a light in it and it locks up. I could let you have the spare key and you could keep your stuff there and get to it whenever you want, until you find a place of your own.' She swayed away to look at him. 'How's that?'

His head shook. 'Your mother might not like it.'

'She needn't know,' Alison said impatiently. 'She's out all day, anyhow. And once she's home for the evening this time of year she stays inside the house. She never even *looks* at the garage. You could come and go and she'd be none the wiser. If you felt like it, you could work there.'

'And have you criticizing as I went

along?'

'As if I would!' she said vehemently. 'I do have some respect for people's privacy. As far as I'm concerned, you could regard the place as your own.' A thought struck her. 'Even if you got fixed up with somewhere to live, you could carry on using it. Treat it as a studio. Why not?'

'You make it sound feasible.'

'It's common sense. The garage is simply going to waste at present. It might as well have some use made of it.'

'If you say so.'

'How long will it take you to pick up these cases? Can you be back here with them by twelve-thirty? That's when I go to lunch. We'll get the bus along to the house and you can have the garage key and dump them there.' She beamed up at him. 'End of problem.'

Her fingers tightened about his shoulders. Resting the side of her head against his chest, she began to tremble with some violence. 'Sorry,' she said, her voice muffled. 'Just relief, really. Thought I'd lost you. After I left you the other night...'

The entrance bell clanged. Freeing him, she did something to her hair, her face averted. Taking a breath, she left the concealment of the recess and picked up a garden fork. 'It's the only kind we stock,' she said clearly. 'If you wanted something with longer prongs, we'd have to order specially.'

'I'll think about it,' he said, 'and come back.'

With a nod to the fresh customer, he left the shop. Walking to the nearest Tube station, he travelled to King's Cross, where he collected two locked suitcases from the left luggage and took them into a buffet bar.

Keeping them beneath his knees, he ate two doughnuts while scanning a copy of the *Examiner* that he had bought from a bookstand. Its front-page lead story concerned a Bill on taxation. Inside, on the Home News page, details were given of the new, tightened-up precautions coming into force in theatres, cinemas, department stores and other establishments in major cities against infiltration by bombers. There was also a situation report on police investigations, underpinned by a special feature compiled by the newspaper's crime team and headed *What Price Safety?*

He read attentively through the page. Anchoring the foot of it was a three-column item in bold face, carrying the information that model-girl Trisha Clarkson, sole survivor of the Grill Room blast, was making good headway and would be leaving hospital within the next few days. A return to modelling? "I'm not thinking too much about that," she was quoted as saying. "I just want to get home and rest for a while, take things easy by myself." Her Fulham address was then given in full.

Tearing out the page, he folded it carefully into an inside pocket of his jacket before resuming his study of the edition.

On the back page, above the daily strip about the exploits of a dog called Wagsie, another news item took his eye. The body of a man, it said, had been discovered by children playing in a derelict house in Peldon Close, Wood Green, that was scheduled for redevelopment. Death, caused by a savage attack with an empty Irish whiskey bottle, had occurred some days previously. No motive was immediately apparent. The man had still to be identified.

Leaving the newspaper beside the plate, he picked up the suitcases and, without haste, left the buffet to head for the Underground.

'This,' Ginny explained, 'would be the bedroom, and this...' She led the way across a corner of the landing. '...could be a sort of lounge-breakfast room or whatever you like to call it. Or you could use them the other way round. I only suggested that one as the bedroom because it's away from the street. Not that there's much traffic noise, as a rule. The occasional motor-bike.'

Ferguson stood looking. His crisp ginger hair glinted in the late November sunlight that crawled through the panes to bestow a fain refulgence upon the yellowish wallpaper. 'As you can see,' Ginny gabbled, 'this gets the morning sun, but later on it moves round to the other window, so there's the chance of a double...'

She pulled herself up. Running a palm

across her hair, she turned to face him. 'Of course, it may be nothing like the accommodation you had in mind. If it doesn't suit you, don't hesitate to say so.'

'On the contrary, Mrs Holt, it's fine.'

'My friends,' she smiled, 'call me Ginny.'

Without replying, he wandered across to the bay window and peered along the street. 'The outlook beats the one I've had for the past two years.'

'Does it?' she said, helplessly.

He pivoted slowly. 'I wouldn't be here an awful lot. I'm out a good deal, as you probably know.'

'There's nothing you can tell me about Squad working hours. Anyway it's not important. You could always—'

'I'm currently tied up with a special enquiry.'

'Yes, I know.'

'So, to be perfectly frank with you, my movements are somewhat unpredictable.'

'That's all right,' she said awkwardly. 'I'm used to it. I quite understand.'

Returning part of the way to her, he stood pondering the furnishings. She followed his gaze. 'Do you have much stuff of your own?'

'From a hotel room?' he asked, with a certain irony.

'I was thinking, you might prefer somewhere with more—'

'This will suit me.'

'You're sure?'

'When can I move in?'

She gestured feebly. 'Any time you like.'

'End of the week?'

'Fine. We'll give you a hand with your—'

'Not necessary. I can manage.'

'Right. That's settled.' She found herself adopting his own staccato approach to the negotiations. 'Like a cup of coffee?'

He glanced at his watch. 'I've just time.'

Downstairs, she left him in the living room at the rear of the house while she went to prepare the tray. When she returned from the Kitchen he was standing with pocketed hands, studying the garden from the double-glazed sliding door that she and Bob had had installed in place of the original festering french window. Without looking round, he said, 'Reminds me of the place I was brought up.'

'Really? Where was that?'

'When I say reminds me, there was a view rather similar to this from the sun-lounge, only of course more extensive. Nottinghamshire. We had this listed building, Grade Two.'

'How lovely.' She added cream to the coffee. 'Is it still in the family?'

'Not now. My people were in property, so they tended to move around a bit.' He took the cup from her. 'Thank you.' The acknowledgement had the gravity of an official presentation. Hiding her amusement, she attended to her own requirements from the coffee-pot.

'You'd no urge to go into property yourself?'

He gave an abrupt shake of the head. 'Not for me. No challenge. I like to have something I can tackle in a cerebral way.'

'I should imagine,' she suggested, joining him at the glass door, 'you've found one of the best possible niches for that.'

He seemed to weigh the proposition carefully before delivering a considered reply. 'There's quite a lot of job-satisfaction. One can give rein to one's capabilities. If one fails, one has only oneself to blame.' The prodigal use of the royal impersonal pronoun made Ginny want to shake with laughter. 'Take, for instance,' he went on, moving slightly away as though sensing the vibrations, and turning to keep her in view, 'this latest outbreak. It's obviously the work of a remarkably clever individual. It's got the whole Squad pinned down. Your brother's told you, no doubt?'

'He doesn't have to tell me. Now and again I wave him off, then sit back for a few days till he turns up again. I expect it's the same with you.'

He took three or four brief pecks at the coffee. 'I'm on special assignment.'

She tried to decide whether this was as self-important as it sounded. In view of his manifest professionalism, it seemed charitable to give him the benefit of the doubt. She said gravely, 'That must make demands on you.'

'Nothing that can't be handled.' Again, it was perhaps less a boast than a statement. She sensed hidden power in his make-up. 'Certainly it's time-consuming, but the outcome should make it worthwhile.'

'I do hope you'll get a conviction.'

'I'll get one,' he said confidently.

She had meant the Squad as a whole. Obscurely irritated, she said, 'Won't you sit down while you drink that?'

'I must be off.' Draining the cup, he handed it back to her. With a docility that she found puzzling, she transmitted it to the table. His manner was faintly hypnotic. Useful, she surmised, in the interrogation of suspects; or did his approach vary? On an impulse she said, 'Bob hasn't told me a great deal about you. Have you worked together much?'

'Very little.' Ferguson was zipping up his padded jacket. 'We each have our own way of going about things.'

'I see.' She couldn't resist adding, 'And you think your way's the best?'

He replied coolly, 'I know it is.'

This time her laughter was uncontrollable. 'Perhaps I'd better not tell that to

Bob.'

'If I might suggest,' Ferguson said unsmilingly, 'I'd be exceedingly careful about saying anything to anybody. Not excluding your brother.'

She gazed at him open-mouthed. Finally she managed another laugh, an edgy one. 'I've been the sister of a cop for quite a while now, Desmond. If I haven't yet learned not to blow the gaff, I doubt if I ever shall.'

Without comment, he walked out of the room. Simmering gently, she followed him along the hall to the street door, allowing him to open it for himself, which he did with efficiency. From the doorstep, he looked back.

'Friday morning, then. No need to wait in for me. I'll pick up the key from your brother.' About to make for his car, he paused. 'I wasn't fooling,' he said quietly. 'I meant every word about that. In this business, you never know who you can trust.'

She stood watching while he drove off. He took no further notice of her.

Frowning, she went back into the house. Passing the open door to the diner, she glanced in at the framed citation hanging on the wall. From the hall it had looked askew: in fact, she found, it was nicely upright. Returning to the living room, she collected Ferguson's cup and took it out to the kitchen to rinse. She switched on the radio, finding the classical music programme and turning up the volume to balance the splashing of water. While she was drying the cup its handle broke off in her fingers.

CHAPTER 13

The duty sergeant advanced with his usual stately benevolence. Outwardly he was tranquil, but instinct was nudging him. He recognized potential awkwardness when it stood up for inspection.

'Yes, madam? Can I assist you?'

'I'm hoping I might assist *you*.

God above, Sergeant Freeman groaned to his soul. It was worse than he had feared. She'd heard a child's cries from the next house. Banging sounds. She was sure they were beating up their three-year-old. She'd never trusted that stepfather. He'd a funny look in his eye, and on one occasion she'd noticed the cat...

'Help from the public,' Sergeant Freeman intoned mechanically, 'is always welcome. What's it in connection with?'

Parting the jaws of a crimson handbag on the counter, she extracted a Press clipping. 'This.'

He turned the sheet sideways, angled his head. 'From the *Echo*,' he observed. He stiffened. 'You've some information to give on the matter?'

'I might have.'

Her lips closed with a smack. Eyeing her obliquely, Sergeant Freeman glanced again at the newsprint and came to a decision.

'If you'd care to step this way, madam...' He lifted the flap. 'I think someone in CID might like to hear from you.'

On arrival Cullen was shown directly to the CID room, where a fresh-faced detective-inspector was in earnest communion with a woman. Of late middle age, she appeared to have undergone a facial wringing and drying process that had subtly distorted the fabric without actually stretching it out of shape: everything was in place, but the total effect didn't quite come off. At Cullen's entrance, she turned to examine him. Her expression brightened.

'John Emerson?' he asked shaking hands with the young inspector. 'Thanks for wasting no time. This is Miss Manning?'

Accepting the chair that Emerson dragged over, he sat facing her. 'I'm Chief-Inspector Harold Cullen. Can you tell me, in a few—'

'Miss Manning,' interposed Emerson deftly, 'keeps a small block of bedsitters here in Wood Green—Wallis Grove—which she rents out. One of her tenants, name of Wood, has just quit. Gave no notice. Simply stuck a note through Miss Manning's door and vanished.'

'When?'

'Yesterday. That is, he—'

'The reason I thought it was queer,' said Miss Manning, loudly, 'is that only the day before I'd asked him if he was planning to leave and he said he wasn't.'

'How long,' asked Cullen, 'had he been with you?'

'Five months.'

'Do you know anything about him? What he did?'

She sucked at her teeth. 'He was apt to keep himself very much to himself. All I do know is, he tended to come and go. He never—'

'You mean, he was in and out a lot in the course of the day? Or there were times when he wasn't there at all?'

'That's right.'

'Which?' Cullen said patiently.

'Times when he wasn't. Two or three days at a stretch, it might be. Mark you, he was regular with his rent.'

'When he was in occupation did he go out much?'

'A good deal in the evening, it seems,' Emerson cut in. 'Several hours at a time. Nearly always with a briefcase. One of the square-cornered executive type.'

'Other times,' said Miss Manning, shouldering her way back, 'he'd be holding a plastic carrier.'

'What did he do for meals?'

'Ate out, I imagine. He'd a cooker in his room—all my residents have cookers—but to my knowledge he never used it. Just boiled up water in the electric kettle for his drinks.'

'While he was indoors have you any idea what he did to occupy himself?'

'He used to play music.'

'Pop stuff?'

'Classical, mostly. Turned up loud, on

his transistor. I did have occasion to mention it to him, once or twice, in a tactful way, you know. He was quite nice about it, promised to keep it down a bit, though I can't say as I ever noticed any difference. But we never had *words* about it.'

'So there was no reason for him to have taken offence. And in fact he'd told you, the night before last, that he'd no intention of leaving?'

Miss Manning settled herself. 'So he led me to understand. That was just before he went out, carrying his briefcase as usual.'

'Did you see him come back?'

'I did, as it happens. I'd been watching a film on the television, and when it was over, about ten to eleven, I went out into the front hall to check that all the lights were off except the one that stays on all night, and just as I was doing that, in he came. The sight of me seemed to give him a bit of a start. I think he'd been hoping not to see anyone.'

'Anything unusual about him?'

'Only that...' She paused.

'Tell the chief inspector,' Emerson

prompted.

'Don't rush me, young man,' she said severely. 'What I'm trying to say is, he looked much the same in himself, near as I could tell in the light: it's what he was carrying.'

Cullen studied her. 'And what was he carrying?'

'Now, that I can't say, not for certain. He was doing his best to hide it from me, like, behind the briefcase on his other side. It looked like a big wrapped bungle of some kind.'

'A bundle of what?'

'Might have been clothes. I'm sure I caught a glimpse of a pair of shoes. Wrapped in plastic, they were. Sort of a big plastic bag.'

'Did he say anything?'

'Just "Good night, Miss Manning." Then he went upstairs.'

'And that was the last you saw of him?'

'Not quite,' she said, with enjoyment.

'When was the next time?'

'While I was getting breakfast the next morning—that's yesterday—I heard my letter-flap rattle. When I went out, there was this note lying on the mat, saying he'd been called away unexpected and he was having to vacate the room. Since he'd paid a week's rent in advance, I wasn't—'

'Do you still have the note?'

'I opened the door,' she continued, disregarding Cullen's intervention, 'but he'd gone. So then I went outside to look down the street, and spotted him just before he turned the corner. He'd a suitcase in each hand, so I could see he wasn't coming back.'

'He'd taken all his belongings?'

'Everything's gone that he had...not that it amounted to much.' Pulling an envelope from her coat pocket, she handed it across with dignity. 'There's the note.'

Cullen read it through, then passed it to Emerson. 'All right, Miss Manning. You've given me the background. Can we get around to the specific thing that brought you in here this morning?'

Rising swiftly, Emerson collected something from his desk and brought it tenderly across. 'Here's the item, sir. Miss Manning did handle it a little, naturally enough.'

The postcard, resting on the inspector's blotter, was creased down the centre and smudged with dirt. One end was frayed, and dirtier than the rest. The message borne by the card was in black ink, spaced out with evident attention to visual felicity, and unfinished. It was in block letters.

THIS TIME THEY'LL BE DANCING TO ANOTHER TUNE. NEMESIS AWAITS. STAND BY FOR

'Other side's blank,' said Emerson, anticipating the query.

Cullen turned to Miss Manning. 'Where did you find this?'

Self-importantly she rearranged herself once more. 'After I'd watched Mr Wood out of sight, I went back up to his room to see he'd left it all in order. As a rule—'

'And had he?'

'Neat as a pin,' she said, with a snap of the lips. 'That's to say, he'd not dusted, but everything was in its place and he'd not taken a thing that didn't belong to him and there wasn't a lot needed doing apart from a good clean-up, which is what I got straight down to..'

Cullen gave the inspector an expressionless glance. 'How far did you get?'

'I'm coming to that. I got the furniture into the middle of the room so I could lift the carpet—'

Cullen jumped up. 'It would save time, Miss Manning, if you could show us.'

'This is it,' said Emerson.

During the five-minute drive, Cullen had learned from Miss Manning that normally she had five residents, two on the first floor, two on the second, and one on the third—a converted attic. At present she was down to three, one of the second-floor apartments having been unoccupied for a fortnight. At this rate she was barely paying her way. These days you had to be careful who you took in. Not that the law let you pick and choose, exactly. She'd a coloured gentleman on the first floor and to be quite honest she'd no complaints about him, none whatever, he paid his rent faithfully and kept himself quiet, but to be candid she'd had less happy experiences with others of his race, and so before making a room available to anyone she did her best to carry out a little unofficial vetting, did the chief inspector understand what she meant? She didn't like it, but in her position...Mr Wood? Oh, she hadn't thought it necessary in his case. He was obviously quite a gentleman. She'd known instinctively he wouldn't create a nuisance.

'But he did play his radio rather loudly, you said.'

'Not so as you could call it a disturbance. I'd no complaints from the other residents, though as I say I did just mention it to him once or twice, as a precaution like.'

'Did he talk with an accent?'

Miss Manning thought not. He'd a deep way of speaking, gruff, you might say; but dialect...no, she couldn't put a finger on any. How tall? She'd had to look up to him, and she measured five seven and a half in her stockinged feet. Oh, easily a six-footer. Dark hair, worn long around his ears and down over his neck. A neat dresser. What with that and the briefcase, she'd put him down as a rep. of some kind: someone who needed to make an impression.

Wallis Grove was chocked with parked vehicles. Ninety per cent of the tall, terraced properties of which the street consisted had been converted into flats or bedsitters; the remaining ten per cent were private hotels of a remarkable seediness. Inside her front door Miss Manning selected a key from a number on a chain inside her pocket before leading them upstairs. By the second landing Emerson, a man of a certain bulk despite his youth, was beginning to puff. The third landing had a slanted ceiling and a solitary door which Miss Manning opened in a clatter of steel.

'You'll have to excuse the mess. As I say, I was just about to—'

'Perhaps,' said Cullen, 'you could point out the place to us.'

With a toss of the head she skirted the furniture. On one side of the room, a section of the shoddy corded carpet had been rolled clear of the wall: the exposed floorboards were chipped and scarred, in one or two cases failing to make contact with the skirting. The arthritic index finger of Miss Manning hovered over the area like a hunchbacked wasp. Cullen glanced at her.

'There?'

He crouched for a closer look. Miss Manning said forgivingly, 'That's where the cupboard was, that he kept his kettle on. When I moved it out and shifted the carpet, that's when I saw the end of the postcard sticking out.'

'Must have dropped behind the cupboard,' theorized Emerson. 'Then slipped down between the end of the floorboard and the skirting. The carpet couldn't have come right up flush with the wall.'

'How much of the card was showing?' asked Cullen.

Miss Manning sniffed. 'About a third of an inch. Wonder to me it hadn't gone right through.'

'Held by the ceiling underneath, probably. The wonder to me,' echoed Cullen, addressing his remark to Emerson, 'is that he didn't retrieve it himself.'

'Maybe he *hid* it there, sir.'

Cullen shook his head slowly. 'Obviously he was in the middle of writing it. Printing it, rather. Then he must have been called away—the kettle boiled, or something—and the card slid off, as you said, and to all intents and purposes vanished. When he came back to finish it and found it missing he couldn't think what he'd done with it. He may have looked all round the cupboard and over the floor, but it didn't occur to him to lift the carpet. Hardly surprising. The way it popped into that gap was pretty freakish.'

'All the same, sir. With potentially incriminating evidence like that, you'd think he'd have taken the room apart.'

'Not if it was at the start of his campaign, perhaps. Before he'd achieved... what he has. At that time, he might not have been so ultra-cautious.'

'Possible.'

'Besides, it probably never occurred to him that if he couldn't find the card somebody else might. After a while he may have completely forgotten about it. Presumably he had a stock of postcards and simply used another one for that particular message.'

'Much the same wording, isn't it?'

Cullen nodded. 'More or less identical to the one sent to the Fulham newspaper.'

'Same hand?'

'We'll soon find out.' Cullen rose abruptly. 'And speaking of taking rooms apart... Is there a telephone here, Miss Manning?'

'Downstairs,' she said apprehensively. 'You're not thinking of causing any damage, I hope. I shall claim compensation, you know. I can't afford—'

'Don't worry. It'll be restored to the condition it was.' To Emerson, who was trying unsuccessfully to conceal a grin, he added, 'Stick around here, would you, while I get things organized.'

Miss Manning pursued him to the ground-floor hall. 'How long,' she demanded, 'before I can put the room on the market again? It's affecting my livelihood, you know. Standing there empty. If I'd known there was going to be all this fuss—'

'You'd have acted in the same public-spirited manner,' Cullen informed her, dialling.

While she was unravelling this, he

issued some low-voiced instructions into the mouthpiece, concluding with a brisk 'Hurry it up' before replacing the receiver in time to detain her before she flounced through her own door and shut it in his face. 'You're not thinking of walking out on me?' he asked, amiably. 'You're our star witness, Miss Manning. We're depending on you.'

'I've a lunch to cook.' Mollified, she came back. 'But I could do coffee for you and the other gentleman.'

'How kind. We might take you up on that. First, though—'

'If you don't mind instant.'

'The faster the better. First, I want you to throw your mind back and tell me everything you can remember about Mr Wood. Appearance, habits, things he may have said to you. The smallest detail could be vital.'

She beckoned him through. 'Snugger in here,' she said, closing the door and trapping him in the furnace. 'Everything I can remember... As I say, he kept pretty much to himself. Not as I'm saying that's anything out of the common, you find this with a lot of single residents, they don't seem to want to get *involved*, if you know what I—'

'Did he have any friends or acquaintances?'

'There again, I couldn't...'

She stopped, her eyes widening in a somewhat objectionable manner. Cullen watched them steadfastly. Something's occurred to you?'

'There was somebody he brought back. One night. A young lady. I was putting out the empty milk bottles and I just happened to—'

'Can you describe her?'

This time the eyes shrank, disappearing into wads of puckered flesh. 'Slim and dark...quite attractive in her way, a bit thin in the face but good hair done in a nice style. Not more than early twenties, I'd say. Of course, the light out there in the hall isn't too good, as I told you before. I just caught a glimpse of her as they went upstairs.'

'Did you hear him call her anything?'

'Only thing I heard him say,' mourned Miss Manning, 'was something about enjoying the evening. He never called her by name.'

'Any idea how long she was here?'

'Barely half an hour. I was just locking up for the night,' she explained, 'when I heard somebody on the stairs and I glanced out and there she was, coming back down by herself. A bit long in the face, she was. I reckon she must've had a car or a taxi waiting outside, because after she'd gone out I heard a door slam and then the sound of a motor, pulling away like.'

'And Mr Wood stayed up in his room?'

'He must've done.'

'There's nothing else you can tell me that might help us to identify this girl?'

Miss Manning looked hunted. 'She was here and gone so quick...'

'Yes, I understand.' At a clatter of footsteps outside, Cullen broke off and made swiftly for the door. 'Attic room, third floor,' he informed the men, slung with equipment, who were tramping into the house. 'Sniffer dogs on the way? Good. You'll find Inspector Emerson up there. Deakin—just a second.'

The sergeant turned back from the staircase. 'I want you to drive Miss

Manning here straight over to CRO. I'd appreciate it,' Cullen told her, propelling her into the hall again, 'if you'd look carefully through the photographs you'll be shown and see if you can pick out either your Mr Wood or the girl...or, better still, both. Don't worry, we'll be here when you get back. Yes, I'm afraid it might take a little time, but if you can come up with anything you'll be the toast of London. That's the spirit. Off you go, then.'

Bundling her into the street, he gave Sergeant Deakin a meaningful lift of the eyebrows and watched the car out of view before returning into the hall. Here he stood momentarily with a look of vacancy on his face, before climbing the stairs to the top floor.

Emerson met him on the landing. Beyond the half-open door subdued but purposeful activity was detectable. 'Something here,' said the inspector, 'that you might like to see.'

Taking it, Cullen said, 'Not another gap in the floor-boards?'

'Not this time. It was screwed up in the waste paper basket under the window.

Struck me it might be helpful.'

'Could be.' Cullen stared at the crumpled receipt. 'Freebottle and Son, The Broadway. Hardware and Household Supplies. Eighty-six pence, VAT seven pence, total ninety-three. Doesn't say what the purchase was. Good work, John. The Broadway...?'

'Half a mile or so in that direction.' Emerson gave a vague jerk of the head. 'Sizeable parade of shops. Like me to pay Freebottle's a visit?'

Cullen glanced towards the room. 'They're going to be happy for an hour or two,' he remarked. 'Let's both go.'

CHAPTER 14

Inserting another nail into the clamp, he hacked off the head before bringing the file up and over in a practised movement, tapering the metal into a point.

Freeing the result, he added it to the heap at the end of the bench, then glanced at his watch. Straightening his back with a slight wince, he walked to the other side of the garage, removed his windcheater from a hook and thrust an arm into one of the sleeves. About to insert the other, he froze.

He stood listening.

The soft scrunching of gravel persisted for a moment, and stopped.

He remained still. Fifteen seconds elapsed. His gaze stayed fixed upon the heavy wooden door, bolted on the inside, top and bottom. There was no window: light came from a neon tube slung from two joists in the ceiling. It emitted a low hum.

Between the first gentle knock on the woodwork and the two that followed, there was a five-second interval. Moving closer, he placed an ear against the door.

'Colin?' Her voice sounded anxious. 'What is it?'

'Can you come outside? Just for a minute.'

He finished putting on his windcheater. With a glance around, he switched off the light and unbolted the door. Stepping out, he shut it carefully behind him.

'I know,' she said apologetically, 'you weren't to be interrupted. But there's something I ought to tell you.'

The chill breeze was making her hair drift. Automatically she thrust it back, looking up at him with a smile that contradicted the worry in her eyes and posture. The fur lapels of the leather coat she was wearing sparkled with the sleet that was starting to arrive from the north-east. Taking his arm, she coaxed him to the other side of the driveway into the shelter of a conifer, one of a line that hid the garage from the house. 'What a morning!' she said, pushing back more

hair. 'Getting on all right in there?'
'I was.'
'Darling, I'm sorry. It's just something that happened this morning, that I thought you should know about. Only a small thing, but—'
'Tell me,' he said, watching her.
'Two men came into the shop. Police officers. They were asking about one of our receipts...'
'Receipts?'
'They showed it to Mr Freebottle and he showed it to me. They asked if either of us could remember who the buyer was or anything about him. And what he'd bought.'
'Were you able to tell them?'
'I could have. It was one of your bags of nails, and the adhesive tape. I recognized the amount and I remember writing it out, a week or two back: I put a tick against the figure...'
'Why?'
'Just a code of my own,' she said, shyly. 'Anyway I remembered quite clearly, but of course I pretended not to. I said I hadn't a clue.'
He said softly, 'And they accepted

that?'

'I don't know. I think so. Mr Freebottle explained how many receipts we dished out in the course of a day and the number of casual customers we dealt with, and they seemed satisfied. But then they said they might be back later with a photo to show us, in the hopes it would jog our memories. Then one of them told us they were looking for a man.'

'Did he describe him?'

She looked at him straight. 'It was near enough of your description. I kept a blank face, and luckily old Freebottle has hardly ever been there when you've come in, so he wasn't much help to them. They left then, and drove off in a car. I waited till I could go for lunch in the normal way and got a bus over here to tell you. I didn't—'

He gripped her shoulders. 'How do you know you weren't followed?'

'I took precautions,' she said proudly. 'I got off the bus two stops early and started walking the other way until I was sure there was nobody taking any interest. Then I came here by a back route. If anyone had been following, I'd *have* to have seen them.'

He looked past her, speaking almost to himself. 'They can get this address from Freebottle. They've only got to ask.'

'But why should they? They've no reason to suppose I've any connection with you. Colin, it's none of my business, but if you're in any sort of trouble—'

'It's my ex-wife.' He seemed to return from a distance. 'She claims I owe her maintenance. She's taken out a court order. That's why I have to keep shifting around.'

'Oh.' Alison considered this. 'And do you owe her money?'

'It's a matter of interpretation.'

She said decisively, 'I don't want to know about it. I've told you what happened this morning: as far as I'm concerned, that's an end of it. I just thought you should be in the picture. Now I must be getting back. Shall I see you this evening?'

'Not this evening.'

'When?'

'I'll be in touch.'

'You're going to carry on using the

garage? It's all right, isn't it?'

'I'll think about it.'

She looked troubled. 'Where are you living at the moment? Suppose I wanted to contact you?'

'Leave the contacting to me.' His embrace left her gasping. 'Get back to the shop,' he instructed. 'If they come in again, do as you did this morning. Act dumb.'

'What else would I be likely to do?' Vacantly she dabbed some hair back into place, dusted sleet-streaks from his windcheater with tender flicks of a hand. 'I wish I could see you tonight.'

'Get out of here. Go the back route,' he added as she turned reluctantly away. 'Keep a sharp lookout.'

She blew him a kiss, took a few steps, turned and blew him another before slipping out by the side gate.

Returning to the garage, he let himself back inside. Closing the door, he turned on the light, walked to the far end, shook out the plastic carrier that lay on the bench and swept into it the mound of sharpened nails, chasing them with the file, the hacksaw and the clamp. From a nearby wall-rack hung a stiff broom. Taking it down, he began sweeping the fragments that littered the floor into a pile.

Above the rasp of bristle upon concrete, something made him pause.

He swung about. The door was partly open, and a figure stood watching him.

'Well, well,' said the voice of Alison's mother. 'How nice to have one's property kept neat and clean. Free of charge.' She rested a hand upon the bench. 'Or perhaps I'm wrong. Perhaps you're collecting payment in some way.'

'That girl at the shop...' said Cullen.

Over the banister rail, Emerson glanced at him enquiringly. 'What about her?'

'Slim, dark, nice-looking.'

'Alpha-plus for observation.'

'But somewhere around beta-minus,' said Cullen, frowning, 'for initiative. I was thinking of nine other things at the time. It's a long shot, but... The Manning female. Is she back yet?'

'I'll nip down and see.'

'I'll nip with you. They're still at it in

there, and they won't want to say much till they've shoved it all under microscopes back at the lab. I might as well keep active.'

'No trace of explosives in the room?' asked Emerson on the way down.

'The dog got frisky here and there, but he didn't turn anything up. Nothing under the floorboards except a dead mouse.'

'Maybe the dog got a whiff of something that *had* been there.'

'Quite likely.' They reached the hall. 'Sergeant Deakin and Miss M not back yet?' Cullen asked the constable at the street door. Making for the telephone, he dialled nimbly. While he spoke, Emerson carried out a critical survey of the embossed paper covering the walls and ceiling, at the culmination of which he exchanged glances of unspecified distaste with the constable. Cullen hung up. 'They're on their way,' he reported.

Minutes later, the car arrived. Waiting until Miss Manning had unlocked the door to her quarters, Cullen wandered in after her, uninvited. A shake of the head from Deakin had already conveyed the message.

'I gather, Miss Manning, you had a fruitless search? That's the way it goes sometimes. Many thanks for trying. You managed the Photofit for us?'

In a drained voice, she said that they had put something together, whether it was a likeness she couldn't say, all she knew was that by the time she'd finished staring at all those pictures on an empty stomach... Cullen patted her solid shoulder and commiserated. 'May I,' he ventured winsomely, 'ask just one more small favour of you?'

She uttered a faint moan. 'Can't I have a bite first?'

'Ten minutes. That's all this will take. Not a second longer, I promise.'

'What do I have to do?'

'Come on a quick trip with us to the shops in The Broadway. You're familiar with them, of course?'

'Not really. I generally catch the bus into town. I'm not much of a one for walking.'

'We shan't ask you to walk,' Cullen assured her. 'At least, no farther than across a pavement.'

He was not quite as good as his word. The distance that Miss Manning had to cover lay between the car's stopping point and the entrance to the hardware store: at Cullen's insistence, one was relatively remote from the other. They watched her trudge away. Cullen murmured, partly to himself, 'Long shot, did I say? More like a moon probe. Still, does no harm to check. God, I'm starved.'

Emerson went across to the corner café and returned with a couple of cheese rolls, one of which Cullen accepted with an appreciative grunt. They were both gnawing when the figure of Miss Manning reappeared, purposeful and rejuvenated. Cullen crushed the remnant of his roll into a side-pocket and wiped his fingers. Emerson climbed out again to open the rear door for Miss Manning. Cullen turned in his seat.

'It wasn't her, of course?'

Miss Manning looked at him. After a maddening pause she said, 'It's her all right.'

His grip tightened on the wheel. 'She's the girl he came in with that night?

You're sure?'

'Positive. I may not have got much of a look at her, but she's got an unusual sort of face, I knew it the minute I went inside the shop. Anyway I recognized her voice. She's the one.'

Cullen sagged a little. 'Thank you, Miss Manning. Thanks for everything. Inspector Emerson will take you home now.'

'And then what?' the inspector enquired in a mutter.

'Then,' said Cullen, with fingers on the door-handle, 'Id like you back here with Sergeant Deakin. On the double. She's seen both of us already.'

* * * *

Removing her hand from the bench, Alison's mother folded her arms.

'Not that I mind people taking advantage,' she remarked, 'so long as I'm in the picture.'

Under the strip-lighting her coiled hair was a harsher shade of blonde. The artificial glare accentuated the furrows that were a continuation of her down-curving mouth, one side of which seemed to be struggling to rise as she looked at him.

'By and large, one does prefer to be aware of what's occurring on one's own patch. You don't mind my mentioning the point?'

The irony sauntered about the walls. He deposited the carrier on his end of the bench, rested the broom.

'Alison said I wouldn't be in the way.'

'Did she now? My daughter has a healthy imagination. It runs in the family. That must be what roused my interest when I spotted her vanishing through the side gate a moment ago. I expect you're wondering what brought me home early.'

She paused, challenging him with a lift of the chin.

'I'm off to Brussels,' she resumed, her eyes scanning the bench. 'A business trip, with my boss. All rather sudden, so I had to come back to hurl a few things into a suitcase; one a little smaller than the two you've got there.'

She contemplated the cases against the wall behind him.

'It almost looks as though you were

planning to move in. Presumably you have a key? All I can say is...' Her head tilted as she re-examined him. '...my fond daughter must be taken with you. Not that I condemn her for that. You're a taking man, in more senses than one. Don't you think you owe me an explanation?'

'She said I could work here.'

'Doing *what*, in heaven's name?' Mrs Duke advanced a step or two. 'You'll have to forgive me for suggesting that you don't appear to have *accomplished* a frightful lot. Apart from a carpet of metal shavings over the floor.'

He nodded at the carrier. 'My work is in there.'

'Ah. May I see?'

'I'm afraid not.'

'How coy. Something artistic?'

'There's an art in it.'

'And so, like every true artist, you wanted somewhere quiet to create in. I can understand that. But I still think Alison might have *mentioned* the arrangement. I'm quite an accommodating lady.' She raised her head to look him in the eyes. 'Had the pair of you asked me first, I wouldn't have felt obliged to interrupt you like this. Would I?'

Receiving no answer, she frowned and touched her hair. 'How long were you intending to make use of the premises?'

'No time limit was set.'

'Oh, it wasn't? That's nice and free and easy. An open-ended contract. What else was included in the small print, one wonders.'

She moved closer. 'Not exactly garrulous, are you? I can't decide whether you're putting it on, or inarticulate. Or whether it has something to do with me. I don't scratch, you know.'

She leaned back against the bench. 'All I want to be assured of is that my property isn't being used for a Nefarious Purpose. Currency forgeries or something. After all, I know nothing about you, do I? I can't be sure that Alison does, either. How long have you known her?'

'A while.' He picked up the broom.

'A shop-floor romance, one might say.'

'I'll finish sweeping up here and leave.'

'Who said you were being asked to go?' Alison's mother placed restraining fingers on the broom-handle. 'Never let it be said I tampered with the pursuit of art. If you want to stay, there are one or two things we have to clarify, that's all.'

'Things?'

'Such as the exact nature of your... work. If it's not counterfeit banknotes, it could equally be something obscene: one would hate to be a party to anything like that. Show me what's in the carrier, and provided I'm satisfied I'll ask no more questions. You can have the place to yourself until further notice. Fair enough?'

He eased the broom away. 'I'll sweep up and get out.'

'Wait a bit.' Her voice hardened. 'I said I thought you owed me an explanation: that still holds. I'm damned if someone is going to stroll in here and make a shambles of it and wander out again without a word or a by-your-leave—no bloody fear, I'm not *that* indulgent. Open the carrier.'

He replaced the broomstick against the edge of the bench. Sliding the carrier towards her, he stood off, watching as she seized the handles and tugged them apart. Her eyes narrowed as she peered inside.

'All I can see is a load of junk. I'm going to take it out, all right?'

With a gesture, he reached for the broom and took it across to its brackets, re-hanging it carefully. In the same movement he lifted down a short-handled, stainless steel shovel. He turned with it in his right hand.

Inclined over the bench, she was removing items from the carrier, distributing them over the pitted wooden surface with a baffled meticulousness.

'None of it looks artistic to me, to be perfectly frank. What possible creative use can you make of a lot of pointed bits of metal? As for the other stuff, I'm not technically-minded but if I had to make a guess—'

From well above head-height he brought the shovel down hard.

CHAPTER 15

Some of the shops, but not all, closed at five.

One of the exceptions was the hardware store. The services of Freebottle and Son remained stubbornly available until five-thirty, by which time cramp had established itself in the leg and thigh muscles of the two inside the car, confirming the onset of an early winter. Emerson stirred painfully.

'Wonder how Deakin's feeling.'

'By instinct, I'd say,' replied Cullen, his teeth chattering.

From the car the sergeant's outline could be discerned, if one knew where to look. The place to look was behind the reinforced glass side of a bus shelter almost opposite Freebottle's on the other side of the street. Since stationing himself there at twilight Deakin had allowed four buses to stop and leave without him.

Previous to that, he had occupied a

telephone kiosk for twenty minutes, hunting interminably through directories for a number. Before that, he had given studious attention to a rack of paperbacks and magazines near the window of a newsagent's premises three doors away from the hardware store, commanding a view of the pavement forecourt. Deakin, in the estimation of his superiors, was putting up a creditable show.

Cullen spoke into the car radio. 'No sign of her yet. The old boy left a minute or two ago. I daresay the girl's responsible for closing up. Customers have tailed off.'

'Standing by.' The Chief's voice was anchored on the monotone that indicated high tension.

'We musn't count on too much,' Cullen warned. 'She could be just a casual acquaintance. Or he might have chucked her.'

'She's the one link we've got.'

'Too right, sir.'

'It occurs to me,' added the Chief, 'that if Sergeant Deakin—'

'She's leaving,' Cullen said crisply.

He and Emerson watched the girl

emerge. After standing briefly on the forecourt, searching her handbag, she snapped it shut and walked briskly the thirty yards to the bus shelter opposite the one presently housing Deakin. She wore a leather buckled coat and a tea-cosy hat, with plastic boots under a mid-calf skirt.

Emerson said approvingly, 'She should be flogging fashions, not beef-mincers.'

'What's she doing?' demanded the radio.

'Waiting for a bus,' Cullen informed it. 'Deakin's joining her now.'

The sergeant had managed his apparently incomprehensible transfer from one direction to the other with commendable aplomb, prefixing the manoeuvre with a sudden anxious examination of the timetable fixed to the shelter, a glance at his wristwatch and a shake of the head as though in self-admonition. None of this by-play seemed to have been necesssary. As he crossed the road and joined the queue, she continued to stare along the street in manifest impatience.

'Seems in a hurry to get home,' Cullen

observed. 'But then, it's a cold night.'

'If we could just have got her name and address...began the Chief.

'We thought of trying, sir. But it meant someone going in and virtually asking, which could have roused her suspicions. This way seemed safer.'

'Also slower. Couldn't you have pumped someone in a neighbouring shop?'

Cullen said restrainedly, 'In the circumstances, we decided a low profile was best.'

'But in the meantime, valuable time is being—'

'Here comes the bus,' said Cullen, thankfully. 'She's getting on. Deakin's close behind. They're both on. We're now in pursuit of the bus. The girl's sitting in the lower deck, somewhere up front...'

'Second seat back,' confirmed Emerson, gliding through the gears.

'Deakin's parked himself at the rear. He's just being handed three yards of ticket. Unless she lives in Watford, that should see him through. We'll keep you informed, sir.'

'I was hoping you might.'

Emerson smirked over the wheel. He had been forced to return to a lower gear to stay in at the rear of the bus, which was proceeding in a series of lurching jogtrots between stops of an infuriating frequency, discarding and absorbing with stately disregard. After the seventh stop, the voice of the Chief said peevishly, 'I suppose she hasn't decided to go visiting a maiden aunt in the Chilterns?'

'If she has, sir,' replied Cullen, grimacing at the inspector, 'we're in for a draughty evening.'

For Colin's sake, she had to think of something.

On first noticing the man as he stood in the bus shelter opposite the shop window, ignoring the buses as they came and went, she had considered leading him a dance in the wrong direction. Then she had thought again. Where would that get her? Eventually she would have to return home, and the man would still be with her. In any case, it didn't matter. She had warned Colin at lunchtime; he would have taken the hint and cleared out, leaving no trace. It was a great pity, but if he was in trouble—and she didn't believe his story about an ex-wife and maintenance payments—there was only one consideration that need concern her and that was shielding him from harassment. Perhaps he was being hounded by a bookie's debt-collectors. They could play rough, she had heard.

Whoever it was, he had to be kept clear of them; but there seemed little point in trying to conceal her place of residence. Leave the contacting to me, Colin had said. Now that he knew they were after him, he would have the sense to make that contact by devious means. All she had to do was wait.

Meanwhile, however, she saw no reason to make things easy for them.

Leaving the bus, she pretended not to see the man seated behind his newspaper on the rear bench. She stepped down on to the footpath and walked back a few yards, waiting for him to get off. When he did so, folding his newspaper and conscientiously dropping his ticket into a litter-bin, she wanted to laugh, although she was also unpleasantly scared. She crossed the road, looking both ways, aware that the man was looking uncertainly about him as though trying to get his bearings. Nobody could be that lost, both ends of a bus journey. Alison's jaw tightened.

Reaching the other pavement, she turned left and lengthened her stride, glad of the loose fit of her skirt.

At the first intersection, she wheeled right and broke into a run.

Reaching the foot of the slope, she glanced back. He was just turning the corner, a hazy shape in the light and shade from the street lamps. Very definitely, he was now hurrying.

Panic seized her. An unnecessary emotion, she reminded herself: but then, how could she be sure that it was Colin this man was after? She might have miscalculated. Taking the first of the optional pair of left turns, she sprinted to the end—a cul-de-sac for traffic, but with a pedestrian outlet between two of the houses. The man in pursuit could hardly miss it, but by getting far enough ahead...

After fifty yards between high fences,

the footpath divided. She took the right fork. A little farther on, she forked again.

By the time she reached the side gate of the front garden, she was certain she had lost him. Even if he doubled back, he had no means of knowing which garden she had let herself into. On tiptoe, striving to keep the gravel quiet, she approached the house. To her left as she passed, she could see that the garage was in darkness.

She felt a little stupid. There had really been no need, after all, for her to have lost her head. The smart thing to have done would have been to take things nice and easily and allow her pursuer to see for himself how empty the house was. And you could say that again. Like the garage, the two-storey structure was black and silent. Her mother was late this evening. Normally she was the first home.

Fumbling in her bag for the door key, Alison hurried up the four steps to the porch and groped for the keyhole. When she found it, the key was upside-down. Uttering a soft 'Damn,' she re-inserted it and pushed the door inwards.

Before stepping inside she turned for a final look, and saw a figure approaching her from the shrubbery.

The exclamation that rose to her throat stifled itself as she recognized the walk. Then alarm flooded back.

'You're taking a chance,' she told him, aware nonetheless of a surge of pure pleasure within her. 'There's someone around, looking for you. And Mother will be home any minute.'

He took her arm. 'Let's get inside.'

'Why did you come back? I thought you were keeping clear, at least for this evening.'

'Something to tell you.' He was urging her through the doorway. 'Don't turn on the light.'

'You're hurting.'

'Keep your voice down.'

With a foot, he slammed the door shut. In the total darkness of the hall she could hear his breathing, sense the voltage surrounding them. Fear stole back. She wanted badly to switch on the light, every light, all over the house.

'Can we have the light on now, Colin, please?'

'Not until I say.' His voice was deeper than usual.

Her own sounded piping. 'Listen...I was followed home. There was a man coming along behind me. Do you think you should stay?'

'I'm not staying.' He was impelling her towards the kitchen.

She resisted. 'Colin, what are you trying to do? Leave go of me.'

His fingers were about her neck. With a sense of disbelief she felt his two thumbs settle against the lump of her throat and exert pressure: sudden, appalling pressure that caused her to gag and retch and throw out her hands. She was being strangled. Strangled by Colin. Such things didn't happen. They were ghost events, haunting the two-dimensional columns of the popular Press. Old Mr Freebottle would die when she told him. Death...

Sagging at the knees, she tried to drag him with her to the floor. She was held upright; held by the throat as though dangling from a noose. She strove to find the floor again. The soles of her shoes brushed the carpet, swung impotently, failing to establish grip. A rag doll. The image rushed unbidden into her clouded mind. Boneless limbs dancing to the shaker's tune. Lolling idiot head. Treatment like this could tear the best workmanship apart.

The manufacturer obviously felt the same. The pressure slackened, lost for a merciful instant the fine edge of its savagery. She found breath to cry out.

Lights inside her skull. Or across and down ceiling and walls. Or everywhere. Uncertainty in the grasping hands.

She thrashed wildly.

Her neck was free, but she was in the way of falling tree-trunks. Comprehension was being beaten out of her.

With fingers outstretched, she jabbed upwards.

In a gulping gasp, the tree-trunks stopped descending. Her fingernails had dug into something soft. She heard wheezing sounds.

She was crawling. There was no plan in her brain, no purpose except that of breaking contact with the falling timber. Through her skirt, the nap of the carpet was rough upon her skin. She heard whimpering, traced it back to source, identified the source as herself. The roughness under her knees sharpened, scratched at her flesh.

Reaching out, she felt the ribbed glass of the front door.

The mountain lay at a distance. Trapped in the foothills, she gathered herself for the impossible: the mountain was ten miles off, immense, unreachable: it was within her grasp, plunging towards her in a rush of frigid air. Staggering forward, she missed her footing and toppled over a cliff.

'For the moment,' agreed Cullen, 'we've lost him.'

The Chief's voice was supernaturally calm. 'You weren't covering the back?'

'There wasn't time.' Cullen's tone remained that of a man stating a case. 'No sooner had we turned in at the gates than the girl fell out of the street door and down the steps. We got straight in after him, but—'

'He'd left. Via the rear.'

'He did have half a minute's start. And there's a labyrinth of gardens and footways over there.'

'As long as the area's been saturated,' said the Chief, sounding more confident, 'he can't get far. How did Deakin manage to lose contact with the girl?'

'No fault of his,' Cullen said swiftly. 'She was evidently on the alert. After getting off the bus, she sprinted away and dived into those footpaths. Deakin hadn't a clue which one to take. He had to ask around, and in fact he struck lucky—first house he knocked at, the owner knew the girl from his description and directed him to the right address. By the time we closed in, though, it was just too late.'

'Girl all right?'

'Throat and head injuries, plus bruising...but mostly severe shock. She can't be questioned for a bit.'

'Another one to project,' the Chief said gloomily. 'Does she have any family?'

'We gather there's a mother who goes out to work. None of the neighbours seem to know where. She's not home yet.'

'Let me know the moment she shows

up. You'd better institute a house-to-house within a half-mile radius. We'll have warnings put out on TV and radio. There's a chance he could break in somewhere, hold a family hostage. Have you considered that?'

'Fully, sir. Somehow, though...' Cullen hesitated. 'I hardly think he'll want to do anything like that unless he's really pushed. He'd know that was the end of the line for him. He'll prefer to stay at large.'

'Possibly.'

'I'll keep you informed, sir.' Cullen's finger hovered over the radio button.

'I'm coming over myself,' the Chief announced, 'to have a look at this place. In the meantime, you've got all the manpower you can possibly need. Make use of it.'

Cullen disconnected. 'Yes, *sir,*' he said to the instrument panel.

Ducking out of the car, he strode across the noisy gravel to the house, now ablaze with light as men searched the rooms. Most of the Squad were on the scene. As he reached the porch, Royce appeared from the flagstone path to one side of the house; he was holding something. 'Harry,' he said.

Cullen paused. 'What have you got there?'

Royce showed it to him in the light of the porch lamp. It was a wig of thick, dark hair, long at the back, with a side parting. Cullen eyed it in silence.

'Where?' he asked, eventually.

'Desmond came across it. Under a bush near the end of the back garden.'

'Terrific,' said Cullen. 'Now we're looking for someone we've no description of.'

'So what's different?'

'I'm getting a hollow feeling Bob, about this character. He's more than just sharp.'

Royce looked down at the wig. 'Shall I have this sent straight over to the lab? Might yield something.'

'A scalp-print?' Cullen speculated. 'Yes, let 'em loose on it. Maybe we can trace where it was bought. Hairpieces aren't my scene, but we're bound to have an expert who can unravel the tangle. And on the subject of tangles, tell the boys in the garden back there to keep at it, will you? Who's there, apart from yourself and Des?'

'Five of us. I've left Des in charge for the moment.'

Emerson appeared at the foot of the steps. 'There's a lock-up garage round the other side,' he told them. 'We can't get in without smashing the door.'

'Smash it, then.'

'Or we could wait for the girl's mother to arrive. She presumably has a key.'

Cullen checked his wrist. 'Turned seven. She could be having an evening out. Show me this garage.'

He and Royce followed the CID inspector to the far side of the conifer screen and down the driveway to the garage's windowless purple-painted facade. Built into the main entrance was a small secondary door. The three of them studied it in silence. Little of the radiance from the house struggled past the evergreens: such light as there was came from the street. Cullen glanced at Emerson.

'How's your lock-picking these days, John?'

'Rusty. I do better with an axe. There might be a key somewhere in the house.

Or the girl may have one on her.'

Cullen frowned. 'Means sending to the hospital to find out. If we could—'

He broke off as a constable approached. 'Sir, we've someone called Philips on the blower. He's enquiring after Mrs Duke. Says he's her boss.'

'*Mrs* Duke?'

'That's right sir. Says he rang several times during the afternoon. Seems she was due back at the office and didn't turn up.'

Cullen raced back to the house. In an alcove of the hall he found the telephone, its handset off the hook. He picked it up. 'Chief-Inspector Cullen speaking. You're asking about Mrs Duke?'

'What the devil is going on there?' The voice of Mr Philips suggested an elegant detachment burdened at this moment by perturbation. 'Has Mrs Duke been burgled?'

'She works for you, Mr Philips, I understand. You were expecting her back at the office...when?'

'Around mid-afternoon. She went home to pick up some things, so that she could fly to Brussels with me this evening. On business,' the voice added, without emphasis.

'And you've not heard from her?'

'Not a word. As it happens, the trip's off. I don't have to go till next week. I've been trying to get through to tell her that, but without—'

'When did you last call?'

'About five. Just before leaving the office. Now, when I finally do get through, all I do is speak to policemen. What's happened?'

'We're not sure,' said Cullen. 'Thanks for phoning, Mr Philips. I'll hand you back to the police constable, who'll take your home and office numbers and we'll probably be in touch.' Passing the receiver across, he shouted an instruction to a man searching the kitchen, left the house and returned to the garage. Royce and Emerson were still there. They looked at him enquiringly.

'We're opening this place up,' he told them.

'How?'

'Mike's bringing something.'

A detective arrived with a steel poker. 'Already dusted for prints,' he assured them. 'Want me to...?'

'Be our guest.' Cullen stood aside.

Inserting the tip of the poker into the crevice between door and frame, the detective applied lateral force which produced bulges in the woodwork and a sound of splitting. Finding a new spot, he repeated the action before biffing the grip of the poker with a beefy palm. The door shuddered but held. He selected a third position, just below the lock.

'Damages out of public funds?' he enquired over a shoulder, and swung on the fire-iron.

The catch of the lock sprang free, allowing the door to fly outwards and hit the detective in the face. 'There's gratitude,' he said stoically, massaging contused flesh.

A uniformed sergeant, who had arrived with him, handed Cullen a flash-lamp. Stepping cautiously into the door-space, Cullen aimed the beam at the nearest wall. A switch was revealed. Using his handkerchief, he flicked it down.

For a few moments, darkness persisted. Then a series of flickers culminated in a 'twang' as the tube ignited, flooding the garage interior with pale white illumination. Cullen stood looking.

Behind him, Royce said, 'What is it, Harry?'

Cullen's voice shook. 'Better get the surgeon here. Fast.'

Leaning against his car the Chief watched as the blanketed mound was carried out to the waiting transport. In the relative silence after it had driven off he hauled a cigar from a buried pocket and with the aid of a gas lighter added a rich aroma to the night air.

'Four hours,' he murmured. 'Cars by the score...police and dogs by the hundred...the full resources of technology...And he's got away. It's impossible, but he's done it.' He turned his head to peer at the hunched figure alongside him. 'How about it, Harry? What's your feeling now?'

'Puzzlement, sir.'

'Is that all?'

'Plus a spot of hopefulness. At least there's been a development.'

'The girl? Yes, if she'll talk. And if she

comes out of shock. And if this bastard doesn't get to her first. He's starting to seem like some kind of phantom, able to come and go as he pleases.'

'His luck must be running out, sir. Apart from the girl, we've some prints and one or two other promising... There's just one thing bothers me.'

The Chief waited, his cheeks exuding smoke.

Cullen squinted towards the rear garden. 'That wig Ferguson found. Seems it was lying under a bush, close to the side fencing...'

'Logical, surely? The bomber chucked it there as he ran.'

'You've not seen the bush. Anything that was thrown from the path couldn't have landed where that wig was found. No way. It would have had to be taken round to the back of it and stowed there.'

'So, that's what he did.'

Cullen's head shook with a slow determination. 'He wouldn't have had time. We were right on his heels.'

The Chief inspected the glowing tip of his cigar. 'What's your argument, then?'

'My argument, sir? I don't have one.'

Cullen turned to get wearily into the car. 'I just can't see how it was managed.'

CHAPTER 16

Alison's throat hurt.

Each time she tried to swallow, everything seemed to contract and grow spikes. She wanted to cry with the pain and the exasperation. Also, somebody would insist on talking. She had no desire to listen. She wished they would clear off.

'Can you hear me, Alison?'

She turned on to her side, hoping that by the time she had to turn again they would have lost heart and departed. But even an ear pressed to the pillow and the other conveyed by a hand was not enough to keep out the voice, the hateful insistent baritone that refused to let her rest. It wasn't her mother's voice. It was male, therefore it must belong to one of her gentleman friends. What was he doing in the house?

'She's not asleep, Commander. Maybe a little drowsy from the sedation.'

'Would you rather we came back?'

'I think she's able to talk. She's out of shock. Let me have a word with her.'

She mumbled into the pillow, 'Go away.'

'You've got a couple of visitors, Alison. Don't you want to see them?'

She twisted herself face downwards, but that hurt her throat and head intolerably. Forced to roll back, she allowed her eyes to focus upon the outline of a face. The fact that she could make out no features grabbed her interest. Gradually, elements sketched themselves in. The delayed outcome was a middle-aged, concerned expression that she found tiresome to watch.

'Well, Alison, how do you feel?'

A senseless question. She closed her eyes. 'Where's Colin?'

Glances were exchanged. Asherton, in response to a nod from the house doctor, inclined himself over the bed. 'We're trying to find him,' he said encouragingly. 'We'd like your help.'

'Downstairs,' she sighed.

'No, he left the house. I expect you know where he was heading for?'

Her head shook, as though under

separate control. 'He wouldn't let on.'

'A house somewhere? Lodgings?'

'I don't know. He wouldn't tell me.'

Asherton glanced back at Cullen, hovering at his elbow. The latter spoke in a whisper. 'Ask her when she met him, sir.'

'How long, Alison, since you got to know Colin? A few months?'

Her eyes came open. 'None of your business.'

'Of course not,' said the Commander. 'I absolutely agree. We're simply anxious to get in touch with him. We'd hoped you might be able to help.'

'How much does he owe you?'

After the briefest of pauses, Asherton said smoothly, 'He doesn't owe us a thing. It was all a misunderstanding. We want to tell him that.'

Alison sat up with a hand to her throat. She coughed a little. 'I don't believe you.' Catching sight of the doctor in his housecoat, her eyes widened. She stared about the room. 'Where is this?'

The doctor, a young man with a startled twist to his eyebrows, advanced to the bedside. 'You had a bit of an accident. Last night. Probably you don't remember.'

She gazed at him. 'Colin was there.'

'That's right. Colin was with you.'

Asherton leaned forward again. 'After your little mishap, Alison, it seems that Colin ran off somewhere. It's highly important that we speak to him. He can help us clear up a few things.'

'Are you the police?'

'Yes. I'm Commander Asherton and this is Chief Inspector Harry Cullen.'

'What are you after Colin for? He never meant to hurt me.'

'We'd like to be certain of that.'

'I've just told you. I should know, shouldn't I? Why can't you leave him alone?'

'All we want from him is a statement. That should enable us—'

'I don't see why you can't take my word for it. Nobody else was involved, after all. It was just between him and me.'

Warning signals emanated from the doctor.

Seating himself on the mattress, Asherton placed an arm against her shoulder blades. After an involuntary hostile twitch, she settled back tiredly into its support. 'Everybody's gunning for him,' she muttered.

'If he does silly things like running off, he must expect to have people looking for him.' The Commander's tone was reasonable, his eyes were kindly as they searched hers. 'He'd make it a lot easier for himself, you know, if he came and had a chat with us.'

'If I *knew* where he was, I wouldn't tell you.'

'But in any case, you don't?'

'He could be in Hong Kong by now, for all I know.'

'Or care?'

The girl was silent.

Cullen had pulled up a chair. He said mildly, 'Considering you're such good friends, I'd have thought he'd have confided in you a little more.'

'Colin's not that sort. You'd have to know him to understand.'

'Yes, I expect we should.'

'For one thing, he's artistic.'

'Really? What does he do?'

'Sculpture,' she said, on a note of

pride. 'He's a modernist.'

'You mean he produces those great circular lumps with holes through them?'

'I've not seen his work. He's close about it. He's a very shy person.'

'Yes, we've discovered that. He told you he was a sculptor?'

'He didn't exactly tell me. I guessed.'

'What made you guess at sculpture?'

'The materials he uses.'

'What materials would they be?'

'Metal, mostly. He buys a lot of nails.' Alison caressed her throat. 'It's sore,' she complained to the doctor.

'I'll fetch you something,' he promised and left the room.

Cullen said, 'How often has Colin bought nails at the shop?'

'Several times.'

'Anything else?'

'Copper wire. That sort of thing. Look, I'm not answering any more questions. It makes my throat hurt.'

Cullen looked silently at the Commander, who looked expressionlessly back.

The doctor returned with a water-filled glass and a tablet. Alison took it without fuss. Ducking out of Asherton's arm, she sank back against the pillow. 'Can't you leave me in peace?' she asked, her eyes closed. 'I want to see my mother. Could you get in touch with her, please?'

Asherton rose. 'We'll have another chat later, Alison. Try to get some sleep.'

'No use trying to rush it, sir,' said Cullen in the corridor.

'Evidently.' The Commander stood fretting, his shoes scuffing the acoustic tiling. 'She'll simply clam up on us. If only we could...'

'We can't, sir. Not yet.'

'No. The doc made that very clear.'

'On the other hand,' Cullen observed, contemplating the statuesque figure of Detective-Constable Barrett who was stationed outside the girl's door, 'at what stage *can* she be told?'

'Ideally, that's a medical decision.'

'But can we afford ideals? While we're stamping around here,' Cullen said in despair, 'the trail gets colder by the minute.'

'Still, at least we now hold a possible ace...if not a trump.'

'But suppose, in the meantime—'

'You said yourself, Harry, it's no good rushing it.'

The house doctor approached. Asherton grabbed at him. 'Mr Pemberton, we do appreciate the situation regarding Miss Duke, but we were just wondering...'

The doctor's head was already moving from side to side. 'Tell her now,' he said, 'and there's no knowing the effect it might have. I can't permit it.'

Asherton looked at him. 'I could go back inside there and tell her myself, this minute.'

'There's not a lot I could do to prevent you,' Pemberton agreed calmly. 'But if you want my opinion, you'd be putting her back—and therefore yourselves—by several days at least. Are you prepared to take the risk?'

'How unacceptable do you think it is?'

'That,' said the doctor with a slight smile, 'I think I must leave to you to decide.' Walking away to the T-junction, he turned left and vanished.

Cullen stared after him. 'Smooth bastard.'

'He's just doing his job,' conceded the

Commander. 'And he could well be right. For the sake of a day, we could lose a week. I suggest, Harry, we come back this afternoon and consult him again. By that time she may be in better shape to...know the worst. Besides Barrett, who do we have on the door?'

'Deakin, who's on next; Ferguson, and Scott, who's worked with Boby Royce a couple of times.'

Asherton grunted. 'I want these corridors covered as well. Yes, I know. The name of the hospital hasn't been publicized and in theory there should be no chance of the bomber finding out where the girl is. But he's shaken us before, and this is one chance I prefer not to take.'

Royce said, 'Why don't we tell her he's wanted in connection with a bank hold-up?'

Cullen gave a jerk of the head. 'Probably give him more glamour in her eyes. He's well under her skin.'

'After what he did to her?'

'Her memory seems vague about it. Or she's purposely fooling herself.'

'Time we snapped her out of it, then.'

'The quack says no. Too soon. Bob...'

'Mm?'

'Something I wanted to ask you. Two things. First, can you tell your Trisha Clarkson that the scheme involving her is being reviewed in the light of developments.'

'She won't be needed?'

'I don't know about that, but the Chief suggests we hold our horses until we see what the Duke girl comes up with. Nothing's gone out to the media?'

'Not apart from the preliminary item. What's the other thing?'

'It's about that wig.'

'Gone off for tests.'

'I know, but it's something else. The place it was found. There's no question it was at the back of that bush, near the base of the stem?'

'That's where it was lying when Des called me over.' Royce paused. 'Something doesn't tie in?'

'I keep asking myself. How come our villain found the time—and, more important, the resolution—to go all the way round to the back of that bush and shove the wig underneath when there was just a matter of seconds between him and us as we came through the house? Wouldn't the natural thing have been to fling it anywhere as he ran?'

'Maybe he did. Couldn't it have lodged there by chance?'

Cullen scowled. 'Weird things happen, I know, but something like that... Those lower twigs would have had to be lifted bodily. The wig couldn't have just drifted in there.'

Royce gazed sightlessly at the end wall of the Squad room. 'Perhaps he didn't throw it away in his flight. He'd hidden it there previously.'

'Why would he? From what Miss Manning told us, he's been carrying all his essential stuff around with him in suitcases—why bury one wig under a bush? It might get soaked with rain.'

'The other explanation,' Royce said meditatively, 'is that it never belonged to our man at all.'

'There just happened to be a wig lying there that we just happened to find? Come on, Bob. I'll buy coincidence...up to a point. What I'd give my upper teeth to know,' added Cullen, draping himself across a desk, 'is how, with the few seconds' start he had, he managed to shake us off. There must have been twenty of us on the scene almost immediately.' He mused for a few moments. 'Which way did you arrive from?'

'West London. I was driving out to see this tame villain of mine for the third time when I got the call, so I came via Swiss Cottage. From that direction, I reached Oakhurst Avenue the opposite end to you. The only living souls I saw were a couple of boys on bikes.'

'How many of the others approached the same way?'

'I could find out. Want me to?'

'Hardly seems important now.' Cullen chewed his lower lip. 'It doesn't make sense,' he muttered.

Royce offered no comment. 'What's the schedule,' he asked, 'with Alison Duke?'

'Commander's having another go at her later today.'

'Her protection's cast-iron?'

Cullen regarded him broodingly. 'We think so,' he said. 'Still reproaching yourself, Bob, over Julie Morris?'

Royce shrugged. 'One hopes to learn from mistakes.'

CHAPTER 17

The voices echoed softly about the shop. When she emerged, however, from the cubicle where the garden tools were stored, Alison found no customer in sight. The shop's interior was mainly in shadow. She was almost sure she was alone.

The light-switch eluded her. Her fingers groped desperately. The density of the gloom made it imperative to find a source of illumination. The voices kept on. If they belonged to customers, she ought somehow track them down, offer her services; but in darkness it was difficult to fix upon a route. Any second she would collide with something, send it crashing to the floor.

Although the words were unintelligible she knew the voice. The calming effect it should have had was lost in the discomfort she felt, the painful blockage in her throat. But for this she would have gone forward. Instead, she tried backing off to the rear of the premises, but there were things in the way, obstacles that couldn't be felt and yet could cause disaster. The voices became louder. From the front window, a slit of light broadened and swelled, rushed at her in a torrent. She shrank back. A sack of peat fell against her head.

'Is she awake?'

Old Freebottle would never say a thing like that. Staring upwards, she identified the features. Beyond them she could discern those of the younger one; he was watching her intently. She had the feeling that there was somebody else, a third person, inside the room. She tried to stop blinking.

'You woke me up. Have you brought Colin?'

Asherton reclaimed his position on the bed. 'No, Alison, we've not contacted him yet. What made you think we'd brought him along?'

'I thought I heard his voice.'

She saw a look travel between the Commander and his colleague. There was a third one, she now saw, standing near the window. Not the doctor. Unless it was a different one, newly on duty. Who cared? They were going to ask her questions.

'I was dreaming,' she added, in a futile effort to pre-empt the inevitable.

'About Colin?'

'I can't remember. You're not going to ask me about dreams?'

'Only if they're relevant.' The Commander's twinkle was unconvincing. 'Tell me now, Alison. Have you thought any more about what we were saying this morning?'

'No. Why should I?'

'I was hoping you might have decided you want to help us.'

'If I did, I couldn't.'

'You wouldn't be willing to look at some photos?'

'What do you mean?'

'We've some pictures of faces. Now, if you could point out one that resembles your Colin...'

'You don't even know what he looks like!'

The Commander's twinkle evaporated. 'If we knew more than we do, Alison, we wouldn't have to pester you like this.'

'I don't see why you do have to pester me.'

'Because the matter's vital. Not just to you and me—to a great many people. Now look. I don't want to upset you. You're still feeling the effects of your accident, and the doctor says you should take things easy. But I have to put this to you. What if I were to tell you that this man you know as Colin—'

Alison covered her ears. Watching him, she saw that he had stopped speaking and was looking up with a gratifying helplessness at the other two. The newcomer, a fair-haired man, seemed to be studying her even more closely than his companions, although with the fading light from the window behind him it was difficult to see his eyes.

'What's our next step?' Asherton was asking.

'The only way we can *make* her listen,' said Cullen, 'is to hold her hands down by force. Which is hardly likely to encourage her to co-operate.'

'We have to get her on our side,' agreed the Commander. 'Bob? Any ideas?'

'Why don't we get the doc to break it to her?'

'He still refuses.'

'In that case,' said Royce, with another glance at the girl, 'she'll have to overhear it by chance.'

Asherton stared. Then his face cleared. 'I'm with you. What's your suggestion?'

'If you and the chief inspector, sir, were to join me over here...'

Paying no further attention to the girl, they did so. On the way, Cullen switched on the light. Royce said in an undertone, 'She's still stopping her ears, but give her a minute. I recommend we keep talking fairly quietly to each other about nothing too important. When I give the signal... How are enquiries going?'

'We're up against a blank wall,' Cullen replied, softly but distinctly. 'Unless there's some kind of a breakthrough soon, we're liable to find ourselves in the position of having to wait for chummy to make the next move. Which isn't a good option. Any comment, sir?'

'Only that you seem to be doing as good a job as you can in the circumstances.' The Commander kept his gaze on Royce's face. 'How about the prints found in the bedsitter?'

'All of them were his landlady's. From the look of it he wiped the entire room clean before leaving.'

'Damnably thorough. Same apply to the garage?'

'We're still running checks, but it looks like it. Nothing on the shovel handle. The other surfaces had been well dusted, too.'

'Footprints?'

'Concrete floor, which he'd apparently swept. As for the gravel outside the house, we'd managed to carve that up properly with car-tyres and our own feet.' Cullen paused. 'None in the rear garden, either. There's a cement path which he obviously used.'

'In any case,' said the Commander, 'a footprint would only tell us what we already know—assuming his foot size matches the rest of him.'

'Whereas a finger-dab might have been some help. But only if it was on file.'

'The fact that he went to so much trouble to clean up after him,' Asherton pointed out, 'suggests that he *has* got form.'

'Or it could merely indicate that he's highly professional.'

Cullen's eyes, like the Commander's, were on Royce as he spoke. Their junior colleague was the only one facing the bed. When he said nothing, Cullen resumed: 'If it wasn't an impossible conjecture, one might almost—'

'The question is,' Royce interposed suddenly, 'where and when is he likely to strike next?'

'People who plant bombs,' said Asherton, seizing his cue, 'don't follow a predictable pattern, unfortunately.'

'There's no doubt now, though, about his identity?'

'None.' The Commander had slightly raised his voice. 'This boyfriend of the girl's, this Colin as she calls him—he's the one who did the bombings, no question. Tragedy is, she won't believe us if we tell her. She'll think we're conning her for the sake of finding him.'

'How can we tell her, anyhow, if she

won't listen?'

'We could write it down,' suggested Cullen, 'and show her.'

'She'd refuse to look. She'd closed her mind to anything said against him.'

'A man who's slaughtered several dozen people?'

'She's not going to believe it, is she? She's not going to allow herself to. I suggest we wash our hands of her for the time being, concentrate on such other leads as we've got.'

'What if we were to tell her about her mother?'

Cullen's enunciation was clear. For a moment the Commander looked at him, and then his eyes flickered towards the door. 'I don't think so—not yet. Why don't we leave her for a bit and chase things up elsewhere?'

'Right you are, sir. You're the boss.'

The three of them made for the door. As Royce was opening it, the girl stirred. 'Hey,' she said.

'Someone'll be with you in a minute, love,' Royce told her. They went out.

Ten yards away from the door, Asherton halted and breathed out between his teeth before glancing interrogatively at the others. 'What do you think? I reckon we've got her on the go.'

Cullen nodded. 'I must say,' he muttered, 'I enjoyed that.'

'We'd no choice,' Asherton said sharply. 'I don't like it any more than you do. It's her peace of mind against possibly the lives of some cinema audience. Question now is, do we let her stew in her juice for a while?'

'Not for too long,' advised Royce.

'A few minutes,' Cullen nodded, 'at the most. Our friend Pemberton's liable to be along any time, crowding us. Who's going back in?'

'Your bedside manner seems pretty good to me, Harry.'

'Any one of us is part of the Inquisition. Wouldn't a fresh face be more effective?'

'Worth a try. Who did you have in mind?'

'There's Ferguson, along there. He's got a persuasive manner, at times.'

'Does he know what's required?'

Cullen beckoned Ferguson to join them. The Commander said, 'I don't know, sergeant, whether you're aware of what we're trying to do...'

'I think so, sir. You want the girl to know everything about her boyfriend, so that she'll talk.'

'Succinctly put,' observed Asherton. 'We hope we've planted the seed of curiosity in her mind: now we want someone to go in and make it grow. Feel like having a shot?'

'Certainly,' said Ferguson, alert.

'All right. See how you make out. Take your time. I suggest you take her a drink or something, without necessarily letting on that you're one of us. Gain her confidence and wait for her to put the questions. I think she's bound to ask about her mother. How you answer, I leave to you. Just bear in mind that we want her...' The Commander cleared his throat. 'Acquainted with the facts.'

'Very good, sir. And if I succeed in that, what then? Do I start putting some questions of my own?'

Asherton hesitated. Cullen said, 'I think so, sir, don't you? Strike while the iron's hot. If she has too long to think about it...'

His superior nodded unhappily. 'Always assuming she's in a condition to talk. I wonder how close she was to her mother.'

'They lived together.'

'That's no yardstick. We're wasting time,' added the Commander abruptly. 'Arm yourself with a glass, Ferguson, and get inside there. You'll find a nurse in that cubbyhole at the end of the corridor. Tell her the girl's asking for a drink. She'll make you something up.'

'Even if we do win the girl round,' said Cullen, as Ferguson went off, 'and she's willing and able to talk...how much is she going to tell us? I don't think she has the faintest idea where he's likely to be found. If he told her anything, it would have been a cover story. The most we can hope for—'

'Identification.'

'Of a sort, possibly. Chances are, she never saw him in anything but one of his wig disguises. She might be observant of physical traits—enough to make it worthwhile showing her the picture gallery. Or she could maybe manage a Photofit, with some hypothetical hair sketched in. His teeth might be recognizably uneven. He could carry identifying marks...'

'Ever the optimist, Harry.' Asherton's smile was wan. 'You're right, though. The more she can tell us, the easier it will be to build up at least some kind of an image. Voice, dress, personal habits... All set, Ferguson? In you go, then. Do your best. If you're in any doubt, or you run into trouble, come out again for instructions.'

'Right, sir. How long have I got?'

'Far as we're concerned, as long as it takes.' Asherton scratched his head. 'It's a question of whether the medical staff leave us alone. We'll hold 'em off as long as we can.'

CHAPTER 18

Alison found the quiet movements of the ginger-haired visitor more restful than the tense immobility of his predecessors. 'Are you one of the doctors?' she asked.

'Some people call me a consultant. I thought you might like something for your throat. How does it feel?'

'Not too bad.' Taking the tumbler, she placed it firmly on the bedside locker-top. 'Are those detectives still here?'

'Detectives?' Ferguson repeated vaguely. 'I wouldn't know. Perhaps they're around somewhere. Don't bother yourself about them.'

'I want to ask them something. Could you get one of them back?'

'I doubt it. Anyway you should rest. When you've drunk that, why not lie back and try and get some—'

'I can't relax,' she said urgently, 'till I've spoken to someone. Can't you find him for me—the older one with the grey hair?'

'What do you want him for?' asked Ferguson, with smiling tolerance. He sat easily on the chair beside the bed.

'I heard him talking to the others. I couldn't make out all of it, but he said something about my mother. I must ask him about it. I tried to get out of bed but I came over dizzy and had to lie down again. Please fetch him for me.'

'I'll try, if you like. But not until you've got that drink down. You shouldn't have tried getting up. You're still concussed.'

Picking up the glass, she took a few sips before replacing it with a shudder. 'I can't manage any more. Will you look for him now?'

'If you absolutely insist. Isn't there anything I can tell you, first?'

'I just want to know why my mother hasn't been to see me.'

Ferguson looked at her. 'That's all?'

'They were saying something about bombings.'

'Bombings?'

'I couldn't hear properly. Do you know what it could have been about?'

'There have been these explosions in London recently.'

'But that couldn't... Are they dealing with those?'

'The detectives you saw? I daresay.'

'Why were they discussing it in here?'

'Maybe some important information had just reached them. I wouldn't bother your head about it.'

'I'd still like to know about my mother.'

'Of course. I'll go and make enquiries. Will you lie here quietly till I get back?'

'Yes,' she said gratefully. 'Thank you ever so much.'

Ferguson closed the door carefully behind him and rejoined the waiting group. Low-voiced, he said, 'It's going to take a little time. I have to tread gently.'

'We know that. I told you not to rush at it. Is she asking questions?'

'One or two. I want to be able to choose my replies—and the time to give them. I was wondering, sir...'

'Yes?'

'Would it be a good idea if the three of

you were to go back to the ground floor for a while?'

'We're quite used to waiting outside doors, sergeant.'

'Yes, sir, but mightn't it draw attention from the staff? If nobody's here in the corridor itself, they'll be less inclined to think the girl's being pestered.'

'Something in that, sir,' said Cullen. 'We might even be able to collar Pemberton, keep him talking. That would give Sergeant Ferguson more time.'

The Commander grimaced. 'I've lost any grip I had on ethics. All right. Let's get down to Reception and look as if we're otherwise engaged. Good luck, Ferguson. Make haste slowly, but don't let a soft heart stand in the path of necessity.'

'Right you are, sir,' Ferguson said correctly.

Waiting until they had passed beyond the T-junction, he re-opened the door and in a business like manner re-entered the room. The girl was sitting up, staring hopefully. Rounding the bed, he picked up the tumbler and inspected it with a slight frown. 'You should have finished this off by now. I'll leave it here, you can get back to it later. Well, Alsion. I've asked around, and nobody seems too clear about your mother's movements.'

Beneath the bedclothes, her body slumped. 'I can't understand it. She must know I'm here. Did you manage to find Mr Asherton?'

'The detective in charge? I'm afraid not. He must have left. Does your mother go out to work?'

'She does, actually.' Hope returned to the girl's thin face. 'Sometimes she has to go abroad at short notice.'

'Then it's possible she's out of the country?' Ferguson sat on the bed.

'She'd have let me know before she went.'

'Perhaps there wasn't time. She might have decided to call you yesterday evening, from the airport. By which time you'd been brought here.'

She moved restlessly. 'I'm sure Mr Asherton's been in touch with her. I heard him mention her to the others. If I could just have a word with him...'

'He'll be back. No doubt with more questions to ask about Colin.'

Her face set in stubborn lines. 'I'm not telling him anything.'

'You don't feel you should tell the police anything you know?'

'He's got it in for him. I can see. He's itching to blame him for all sorts of things he hasn't done.'

Ferguson allowed a pause. 'He sounds quite a guy, this Colin.'

She looked up, suddenly animated. 'He does these incredible sculptures.'

'You've seen them?'

'No, I haven't seen them, but... He uses all modern materials. And he has these marvellous eyes. Visionary eyes.'

'But,' said Ferguson reasonably, 'he beat you up.'

'There was a reason for that. I've been lying here, trying to work it out. He didn't mean to hurt me. They were after him, so he had to... I'm not sure. I think it was to show them I wasn't...his partner, see? So I wouldn't get into trouble.'

'What makes you think he might have got you into trouble?'

She looked at her fingers. 'It's obvious he's under suspicion. He as good as told me. What led up to it I don't know, but it can't be anything dreadful. Not Colin.'

'You believe that, don't you, Alison? You'd go on believing it, no matter what you were told about him?'

The girl stared up at him, and as she did so a new look invaded her eyes. Casually, he continued to talk.

'Even though you know so little about him. Where he lives, what he does: his background. Despite your total ignorance of all this, the fact that he's never confided in you—nothing would make you doubt him?'

Alison gazed at him fixedly.

'We'd prefer to stick around,' Asherton told the doctor. 'That's if we're not in the way.'

'Of course not.' Pemberton, towards the end of a taxing day, remained equable in tone. 'I should warn you, though, there's no chance of my relenting tonight. She's not entirely out of shock.'

The Commander fidgeted. 'Understood.'

'But we appreciate you're anxious about the security aspect. You're keeping someone on the door, I take it?'

'He's up there now.'

'There's a small waiting room over there, not used at night. We can make that available to you.'

'Most kind.'

'Anything more I can do for you?'

'We won't keep you from your patients. Ward rounds from now on, I suppose?'

'Not me,' the doctor said fervently. 'A couple of reports to make up, then I'm off.'

'Ah, that's nice. Thanks for your help.'

Asherton led the way into the waiting room, a carpeted rectangle off the main concourse, furnished with steel and leather chairs and strewn with pulverized copies of *Autocar* and *Farmer's Weekly*. 'We'll sit around here for twenty minutes,' he muttered, 'then do a recce upstairs. With luck Ferguson won't be prematurely disturbed.'

'If he is,' said Cullen, 'he should be able to talk his way out of it. He could say he's had orders to look in on her every half an hour.'

'If that occurs to him.'

'He's quite sharp. He'll think of something.'

'But will he succeed in his primary purpose?'

'That's up to the girl. Depends how effectively we played on her anxiety. God, this is a swinish business. And at the end of it all we might get nothing of value out of her.'

'I can't believe there's *nothing* she can tell us. Bob, what d'you say?'

Royce had remained standing while his superiors sank into chairs. He looked preoccupied. At the Commander's enquiry he gave him an abstracted look.

'Frankly, sir, I'm keeping an open mind.'

'Looks a somewhat absent one to me,' Asherton said appraisingly. 'Something niggling you?'

'There is a small matter I'd rather like to look into.' In reply to the Commander's questioning glance, he added, 'Only take a few minutes.'

'Well, carry on. If we're not here when you get back, we'll be upstairs. Any idea what's struck him?' he asked Cullen, as

Royce left the waiting room.

Cullen was looking perplexed. 'Whatever it is, sir, it must be something he can settle by phone. He'd be gone more than a few minutes, otherwise.'

Several nurses and an orderly or two passed Royce on the stairs. One nurse, a pretty Malaysian, gave him a pert smile. Ignoring them all, he continued swiftly to the second floor. From the top of the stairway, an expanse of floor narrowed into the corridor that gave access to the wards. At the first intersection, a uniformed figure moved forward.

'I'm afraid I must ask you... Oh. Sorry, sir.'

'Don't be, constable. You're doing the right thing. Who's at the far end of the corridor?'

'Butterworth, sir.'

'Good. Stay alert.' Striding on hastily, Royce reached the T-junction and swung right. The door to Alison's room was twenty yards along. Beyond it, double swing doors shielded a public ward, from which a clashing of china could be faintly heard. Apart from this, the floor was silent.

Treading soundlessly, Royce came abreast of the door to the private room, halted, looked around.

Seeing nobody, he placed his right ear to the woodwork and listened.

'You've gone very quiet,' said Ferguson. 'You probably need more rest.'

Rising from the bed, he stood looking down at her. 'By tomorrow everything will have sorted itself out. No problem.'

Her voice emerged on the brink of a gasp. 'I want to see Mr Asherton.'

'I don't believe that's possible. I think he's left the hospital. Why? Is there something you want to tell him?'

'I'd just like—like to talk to him.'

'You can talk to me, you know, just as easily.'

'Please go and find him.'

He sat again on the edge of the sprung mattress. 'I think you're behaving rather childishly, Alison. You keep asking for people who aren't here. I'm here. I'm ready to listen.'

'Mr Asherton's the one in charge.'

'Sure, but he has to delegate. Now

look, let's be sensible. You're tired, you need sleep. Let me plump the pillows for you. Then you can lie back and—'

'Don't touch me!'

She thrust out both arms. Evading her fingers, Ferguson said calmly, 'Now you are getting worked up. Keep still, Alison. There's nothing to get excited about. I just want to help you to sleep.'

She said pantingly, 'Why has your voice changed?'

'Let me have the pillow, Alison.'

She stayed rigid. 'It's your eyes. I didn't notice before. I was wrong about them. Keep away or I'll scream. You want me to scream?'

With a lightning movement he pulled the pillow from under her head. As she tried to roll he grabbed her, held her in the centre of the bed. Fighting down her thrashing arms, he lowered the pillow across her face.

His full weight was upon it. Choking sounds came from beneath. Shifting position, he blanketed her heaving legs, pinned them down while he maintained the pressure. Her struggles weakened.

Behind him, the door burst open. He

glared round, his features contorted. ‘Bloody copper,’ he snarled. ‘Why do you always have to interfere?’

Dodging Royce’s first grab, he swung himself off the bed towards the window, stood crouched with his back to the panes. ‘You want trouble? You want someone to get hurt?’

‘Take it easy, Desmond,’ said Royce.

He was between Ferguson and the girl. Whimpers were escaping from her. ‘Stay where you are, Alison,’ he instructed. ‘Don’t try to move.’

She collapsed into hysterical sobbing. His attention distracted, Royce failed to hold Ferguson as the latter launched himself towards the partly-open door. Gaining the corridor, he slammed the door in his wake. Royce leapt for the handle.

‘Butterworth!’ he roared, wrenching the door back.

Ferguson was vanishing into the T-junction. Royce covered the distance in nine strides, arriving in time to see Detective-Constable Butterworth laid flat by a two handed assault as Ferguson achieved the open space beyond the corridor. Royce sprinted in pursuit. In passing, he shouted, 'Take care of the girl!'

Glancing back, he saw Butterworth drag himself up, shaking his head.

Instead of accommodating stairs, the open space served as a marshalling point for several corridors leading off in various directions. From a distance came the sound of running feet, muted by cork tiling. Investigating the nearest corridor, Royce saw nothing. He tried the next, with the same result. From the third, a nurse was approaching with rapid steps. She looked up, startled.

'Did a man pass you?' he demanded. 'Ginger hair?'

She began shaking her head. Without waiting, he returned to the first corridor and took off at a gallop, passing a series of ward entrances into which he threw glances, until a right-angled turn took him into a narrower passage, flanked on one side by what looked like administrative offices with frontages of ribbed glass, and on the other by sliding windows giving a view across a flat roof to distant trees and house-tops. As he ran, Royce kept watch on the roof and saw nothing.

The passage expired in a blank wall. He pulled up, swearing. Nearby, a door opened and a small neat man emerged in an enquiring stance. 'Is there something I can—'

'Police.' Royce showed his card. 'What's the fastest way to contact Reception?'

'Phone in here,' said the small man, rising with aplomb to the occasion.

Royce spun the dial. To the answering female voice he said, 'Police, emergency. There's a Commander Asherton in the small waiting room. Get him, quick.'

Waiting, he walked in circles, watched with nervous interest by the room's incumbent. Asherton's level voice came through. 'What is it?'

'Royce, sir. It's Sergeant Ferguson. He's our man. He may be on his way—'

'What? Ferguson? What are you talking about?'

Royce snatched breath. 'Ferguson's the bomber, sir. He tried to smother the girl. I chased him but I've lost him. Can we cover the exits?'

The pause was brief but eloquent. 'Where are you now?'

'Second floor. Unless he's holed up somewhere, he'll be on his way down. You'll have to work fast.'

'We'll see to it.' The receiver crashed down.

To the small man, riveted in front of his desk, Royce snapped, 'How many ways out of this place?

'About a dozen. The main ones—'

The man was left talking to the walls as Royce, with a groan, returned to the passage and ran back to the central point. Occupying a corner, he now saw, was the door to a service lift. To his frantic thumbing, the door slid aside. With agonizing deliberation he was taken to the ground floor. Cullen, white-faced, met him at the reception desk.

'We've put out a call.' His voice was shaky. 'In a few minutes the area will be swamped. How long has he had?'

'About four minutes. Our only hope is he's gone to earth somewhere in the building. Is the girl okay?'

'Butterworth's with her, plus a brace of nurses. I'm not believing this yet, Bob.

It hasn't sunk in. Did you suspect Desmond?'

'Not consciously. Look, Harry, he's a psycho, and this is a hospital, for Christ's sake. What's our best plan?'

'Method. No sense panicking in all directions. Once we're organized, we can work through the place.'

'He knows how we operate. What if he—'

'Let's just cross our fingers,' Cullen said tightly.

The Commander erupted into view, pursued by a pack of medical staff and administrators. '...every precaution,' he was saying, 'to safeguard the patients. I won't hide from you the danger that this man represents. He *could* take hostages.'

'I doubt it, sir,' said Cullen, observing the looks of near-panic that passed between the staff. 'Ferguson knows the siege drill as well as we do. He'd realize it would get him nowhere.'

'Still, it remains a factor. Where the blazes are those...'

From outside a concerto of car sirens interrupted him. Cullen headed for the main exit.

'I'll get things laid on, sir,' he said from the revolving door. 'Is there someone who can describe the hospital layout to me?'

A heavy-shouldered man in overalls stepped forward. 'I can do that,' he offered.

'Right. Come along with me.'

As the two of them disappeared, Asherton turned to an elderly, dark-suited man at his elbow. 'I want every available light switched on—inside and outside the building. Can that be done quickly, but with precautions?'

The man conveyed some instructions to others, who scattered with purposeful expressions. Royce watched uneasily.

'Too many bodies around in this place,' he complained. 'Live ones, I'm talking about. Liable to simplify things for him.'

'You're not suggesting, Bob, he came armed with a bomb?'

'I think not, sir. Far as I could see, he was carrying nothing. I'm just saying, in a place like a hospital... Why the hell did I lose him?'

'No fault of yours. You did well, in

any case.' The Commander beckoned Royce into a vacant area of the concourse. 'I suppose there's no possible doubt? He hasn't just gone temporarily off his rocker?'

'If there's a doubt, sir, it's not in my mind. There's only one reason he could have wanted to put paid to the girl.'

'To stop her talking. But how could he have hoped to get away with it?'

'If he could have done it without leaving a mark on her, it could have been put down to respiratory failure. Delayed shock...something on those lines. Anyway, he had to take the chance. While she was alive he didn't feel safe.'

Mystification joined the haggardness on Asherton's face. 'She'd seen him already. Before he came out, I mean, to ask for more time with her. Why didn't she holler then? No, wait a bit. Trying to protect him, wasn't she? But in that case, why—'

'She probably didn't recognize him at first. Up until then, she'd only seen him in his Colin Wood disguise.'

'Why did he need worry, then?'

'Because,' said Royce stolidly, 'he's

the type that has to tidy up as he goes. He has to be certain. That's why he rubbed out Julie Morris. That's why Trisha Clarkson must be high on his list. He's obsessed with covering his tracks.'

The Commander stared at his feet. 'This is the man we've had on the Squad for six years...I'll hear more later.' On his way to the revolving door, he glanced back. 'You sniffed him out, Bob. Do it a second time, will you? Before he adds to our troubles.'

CHAPTER 19

Despite the cramp that was clasping his muscles he remained still.

The temperature was high, and getting higher. The air was stale and the darkness was intense. None of this mattered. It would not be permanent, and besides, disregarding the slow-burning virulence of his anger against Royce, there was amusement to be found in the antics which he knew were in progress all around him. Just for fun he had tried estimating the precise time at which the search would lap closest to his shores: he had been out by a few minutes.

But the fury smouldered; Royce, the Squad plodder! The stifler of initiative! This was the man who had chosen, at a crucial moment, to put out an interfering paw and ruin everything. It figured, in a way. Royce had been showing signs of uppishness for some while. He had earned a sharp lesson.

Once this had been attended to, the Alison menace could be dealt with. After that, the Clarkson girl.

A tidy programme. Everything taken care of, all loose ends secured.

The temptation was to start at once. While they were all back on their heels and rocking, it would be easy enough. Delay seemed pointless.

On the other hand, let them sweat a bit.

Returning with Butterworth to the second-floor lift space, Royce stood in thought.

His companion waited patiently. Free of all ambition to make a name for himself for flights of intuitive fancy, shafts of revelatory brilliance, Butterworth was content to trudge and get there. When Royce pointed to the middle corridor he followed without question.

On their left, the swing doors to every ward were fastened back and guarded by a pair of uniformed patrol-men. Within, nurses could be seen routinely at work; the passing of the two detectives went virtually unnoticed. Nodding to the guards,

Royce walked the length of the corridor, glanced into the children's ward at the end—earning himself a cheer from the more gymnastic of the youngsters—turned and came slowly back, dogged by the detective-constable.

'Seems all sewn up, sir.'

Royce nodded, his features coasting in neutral. A voice came through on Butterworth's personal radio. Responding with a few placid words, he said to Royce, 'First floor's cleared, sir. They're now starting on this one. Reckon we're wasting our time, don't you?'

'Why?'

'If you ask me, he's bunked long since.'

'Odd you should say that. I can smell him, right here.'

For all his serenity, Butterworth's head jerked. 'On this floor, you mean?'

Royce spoke half to himself. 'I can't think he's left the building. The job's not finished.'

Butterworth's silence was ambiguous. He continued to follow as Royce meandered along the outer corridor surveyed impassively by the two men stationed at each end. Back at their starting point, he again stood cogitating before addressing the nearer of the guards. 'Who checked the linen cupboards?'

'I did, sir. With Wilson at the far end.'

'Satisfied with your search?'

'Absolutely, sir.'

'Mind if I check again?'

The constable smiled uncertainly. Returning to the central corridor, Royce halted at the first of the small doors on their right. Butterworth scraped gently at his neck with a thumbnail.

'Shouldn't we wait, sir, for the main party to—'

Royce dragged open the door. A small washroom was revealed. Stepping inside, he looked around and came out. The next door concealed a pantry, equipped with wall-cupboards and a sink. He opened the cupboard doors, exposing crockery which he moved meticulously aside. At the third door, Butterworth said, 'My turn, sir,' and released the catch. Shelves of bed-linen met their inspection.

'Have it out,' muttered Royce. 'The lot.'

Midway through the job they were joined by the main party. Cullen looked strained.

'We're running in tiny circles, Bob.'

'They're the sort that cover all the ground. Chief here yet?'

'Half an hour ago. He and the Commander are eyeball to eyeball. Results, incidentally, from Ferguson's hotel room. He was all packed up ready to leave for your place. Two of the suitcases were locked away in a cupboard. They were full of wigs and other clobber.' They looked silently at one another. 'He's not been seen there,' Cullen added, 'since yesterday afternoon. We've left a couple of men on the spot...just in case.' He glanced around. 'I think we have to face it, Bob. We're not going to find him there, and we're not going to find him here.'

Royce said stubbornly, 'I don't know.'

Surveying the strewn linen, Cullen stepped over it to peer into the closet. 'If they're all like this... You want to clear them all yourself, or will you trust us to do it?'

'I'd like to turn my attention elsewhere.'

Cullen studied him. 'Okay,' he said. 'Stay in touch.'

The heat and airlessness were causing a little trouble, but on the whole he felt good. Challenge had to be met. Not simply met but outrun, left far behind. It was the only way.

The noise of the hunt had long since dwindled and died. But as he was mentally drafting the next note that he would send to the Press, a new sound reached his ear. Approaching footfalls. Only a pair; perhaps two pairs. As they passed, a low-voiced exchange could be heard. Two voices, both recognizable. His fingers tightened.

'This place has been covered, sir,' said Butterworth.

Royce gazed around the boiler-room. The collective glare of the strip-lighting was hurtful to the eyes. 'In that case,' he said, 'you can get back upstairs. I'll just take another look.'

The other looked suddenly doubtful. Royce eyed him quizzically. 'If it's been covered, it must be clear.' Then he added, 'Go on, say it. If it's clear, why take another look? I can't tell you. Can't even tell myself. I'll be right up.'

'Shall I leave you the radio, sir?'

'No, I'll only be a couple of minutes.'

With reluctance Butterworth departed. When his feet had stopped exploding on the concrete steps Royce moved to the centre of the boiler-room and stared around.

At the farther end the three main oil-fed boilers hummed and shivered. Pipes snaked across the ceiling and walls towards them, performing loops and whirls at the points of entry. The atmosphere was overpowering: it was like being face-slapped with hot towels. Skirting the boilers, Royce approached the reserve exit in a corner of the facing wall and tested its security. The heavy bolts were shot, top and bottom.

Back-tracking, he took up a position at the foot of the concrete stairway, one arm above his head and against the door frame, whistling softly to himself.

Presently he walked across to the right-hand wall. At its centre, five feet from floor-level, a metal grille about a yard square was cemented solidly into the brickwork, shielding a recess which housed what seemed to be an air-extractor. Royce brought his face close to the steel.

The sound was slight, barely detectable above that of the boilers. It came from immediately to his rear.

Experience told him to move first, look later. He was in the midst of the first manoeuvre when the incendiary struck.

After the detonation on his left shoulder came the fire. It ran down to his ribs and up into his brain, scorching the tissue. The floor jumped at his face. Trying to avoid it he threw out both hands, felt his wrists buckle as the floor won.

He rolled to his right. Alongside him, something smashed into the cement, creating sparks. Chips of masonry stung his face.

Automatically he kicked out, encountered nothing, kicked again in a scything movement. This time his shoes made contact. He heard a grunt.

Ferguson's eyes glared above his own. For an instant, a frozen fragment of time, they were in deep communion, each telling the other something: then Royce kicked out again, finding the target, feeling puffs of the other's ejected breath against his forehead. The brief offensive, he knew, was inadequate. Rolling again, the opposite way, he was barely soon enough to impede the other's grasp of the metallic object lying in the dust. He brought an arm across, tried to use it to advantage.

In weight terms there was little between them. His handicap was the dulling of reflexes, mental and physical, from the initial blow. He was short of ideas. While he was trying to formulate one, Ferguson broke free, leaving in Royce's grip the length of copper piping, with a jagged end, over which they had been wrestling. He jerked it at the sergeant's mouth. Dodging it narrowly, Ferguson scrambled to his feet and made for the steps.

Dragging himself in pursuit, Royce collected wind for a hoarse shout of warning.

It brought Butterworth at a sprint across the concourse. Blocked from that quarter, Ferguson wheeled in the direction of the radiology department, only to be met by a uniformed trio advancing from an annexe. Veering again, he darted up more stairs to the first floor.

Butterworth spoke into his personal radio. 'Suspect is at first-floor level above X-ray section. Can we have assistance, please.'

Royce took the stairs on tottering legs. Ferguson was heading for the wards. At sight of the guards he changed course once more, making for a passage that skirted the outer wall of the building. Royce was fifteen yards behind. Running, he let out a groan and then another shout.

'Get back! *Get back!*'

A small West Indian nurse had appeared at the mouth of the passage, carrying a tray of surgical instruments. She stood agape as Ferguson approached. He ran heavily into her, spinning her, sending the tray flying. Instruments clattered to the floor.

Ferguson's movements were almost instantaneous. Clutching the nurse, he wrenched her to one side, holding her powerless while he stooped to retrieve from the floor a surgical knife, then bringing her round with the stainless steel edge at her throat. Her eyes rolled, the whites standing out in shock. Royce came to a standstill.

'Stop there,' directed Ferguson. He was breathless. 'Stop right there.'

'Nobody's moving,' Royce assured him.

Ferguson gave the nurse's neck a jolt. 'Make trouble and she's for it.'

'We're not making trouble.'

'Give us clearance, then.'

Royce flapped a hand at those behind him. 'We're standing back.'

'Farther. Across to the other side.'

Royce set an example. The rest, with varying degrees of celerity, followed him to reassemble in a taut, silent file against the opposite wall. In the course of this procedure, running footsteps from the central corridor presaged the arrival of Cullen and his party. Ferguson called warningly, 'Tell that lot to keep their distance.'

Royce shouted. Cullen who was first to appear, absorbed the situation at a glance and gestured his men to a halt in the corridor.

'Nobody,' said Ferguson, 'had better twitch a muscle.'

Slowly he began to move, impelling his captive across the floor space towards the stairs. Her feet slithered on the tiles. But for her wide-open eyes, staring at the ceiling with the fixedness of total horror, she could have been taken for unconscious. The knife stayed at her throat, an inch from the ebony skin.

At the top of the stairs Ferguson turned her so that he could descend backwards, dragging her after him. Her heels plopped from stair to stair. It was the only sound in the building.

Cullen glanced towards Royce, who gave a slight shake of the head.

Ferguson had reached the ground-floor concourse. They heard him give orders; the scuff of his and the nurse's heels; seconds later, the swish of the revolving door. At that point, Cullen grabbed Butterworth's radio.

'Suspect is leaving the hospital main entrance,' he reported, 'with a hostage. Do *not* try to detain him. He is *not* to be approached.'

A voice crackled back. 'We can see them. They're coming down the steps.'

'He's still holding her?'

'Like a sack of bloody apples. What do we do?'

Keep watching. Report his movements.'

'He's lugging her over to one of the cars.'

'Is it manned?'

'No. The keys won't be in it.'

'If he asks, let him have them.'

'If you say so. Hold it. He's calling across now.' An interval ensued. 'Sergeant Kemp's taking them over. He's been told to stop. He's chucking them the last five yards. Now he's on his way back. Suspect's picking them up. He's opened the driver's door...packing the hostage inside. She looks in poor shape.'

'Hurt?' said Cullen sharply.

'I wouldn't think so, but scared out of her mind. He's getting in after her. What do we do? He's starting up.'

'Have another car ready. We're on our way out.'

The surge of the motor, obedient to his right foot, was like the punch of an injected stimulant. He smiled grimly over the wheel.

Through the lot of them, like wire through soft cheese. The ease of it was absurd.

Beside him, the small figure of the nurse sat in a crouch. For practical purposes she was dead already. She could keep.

They were following, of course. The beauty of it was that there was nothing they dare attempt. If he chose he could lead them an indefinite dance all over the British Isles. He hadn't decided yet.

When he did he might let them know.

Rain was starting to fall. He flicked the wiper switch and cleared the screen. Traffic was moderate. He was adhering to the general pace, not trying to hurry. Only amateurs hurried.

On a thought, he switched on the VHF radio. Silence. Again he smiled to himself. Their mental processes shone like beacons. Who did they think they were dealing with?

He drove a little faster.

On his near side a direction sign came up: Hatfield, The North. The road broadened to dual carriageway. Keeping to the slow lane he checked in his mirror to confirm the continued presence of his escort. The gap between them was a respectful furlong. He experienced an almost overmastering urge to throttle back, allow them to come alongside, perhaps exchange some sign language across the cat's-eyes. But when, experimentally, he dropped speed a little, the following vehicle did likewise, maintaining its distance.

With a shrug he picked up the pace.

In the adjoining seat the nurse stirred and gave utterance to a wavering moan.

He tossed her a glance. A seven-stone bundle of quivering ineptitude, a barely human jelly...for the sake of this he was being allowed, if not incited, to do exactly as he liked. So much for reason. There was going to be little fun in disposing of her. It would amount to no more than kicking a sack of mail from a train.

The one small challenge was the timing. She still possessed traces of usefulness. Why rush things?

Hatfield and The North. The white-on-blue lettering glowed in his headlamps and was snatched away. The North. A title with a ring to it. Wild bearded men descending from the hills, rape and pillage, rout and conquest. Dark centuries of barbarism, the rule of force, the pre-eminence of power. Death and Schubert amid the heather. The speed of the car increased. It drifted to the fast lane, leaving the sluggards behind where they belonged. One hand on the wheel. Lean back, enjoy the ride.

When the nurse sat up, he scarcely attended to her.

'Where you taking me?' she demanded.

'Little girls don't ask questions.'

'This little girl does, for sure.' Leaning across him, she stared at the speedometer. In a brief fit of indulgence he let her. Suddenly the car's power died. Deprived of control, he wrenched at the wheel. Her body was across it, hampering his efforts.

By the time he had thrown her off they

were over the central reservation and on course for a bridge support. Although he avoided this, the car spun on the wet surface, hit a steel barrier and overturned. When Cullen and his men arrived at the spot the offside rear wheel was still revolving.

CHAPTER 20

The report was neatly photocopied.

Leaning across his desk, Commander Asherton gave life to the adjustable lamp and projected the beam at the wad of foolscap sheets lying on his blotter. It was after nine-thirty in the morning, but the sun had got lost in the fog. Three months of winter, he thought glumly, still to come. And then the savagery of spring. How could there be an immigration problem?

Rapidly scanning the opening paragraphs, he turned to sheet 2 and ran his gaze to the centre. The meat of any report, he had usually found, commenced about there.

Logistically, the deception was relatively simple to maintain. Two main points should be borne in mind:

(a) Det-Sgt Ferguson's operational rou-

tine
(b) His personal background

With regard to (a), the procedural tradition of the Special Unit is relevant. Personnel seconded to this branch are in general afforded considerable investigative latitude...

The Commander heaved a sigh.

'If what is meant,' he murmured, 'is that Squad members are encouraged to pursue their own lines of enquiry...why the blazes can't that be said?'

So far as (b) is concerned...

Behind the Commander the door opened. Without stirring he said, 'Are they here?'

'Shall I ask them to wait, sir?'

'No, no. Wheel 'em in.'

He was still immersed when the Chief entered with Cullen. He flapped them into chairs.

'Just mugging up on what the experts have to say. So far, they're not telling me much I hadn't already assumed. Before we get started—how's the little coloured nurse?'

'Quite perky, sir,' said Cullen. 'In fact, exuberant. She'll dine out on her exploit for weeks to come.'

'She's earned a buckshee meal or two,' Asherton said tolerantly. 'Switching the engine off under his nose must have taken some nerve, especially at eighty in the fast lane. Thank God she got away with it. What are her injuries?'

'Head lacerations and a few ribs. She'll be fine.'

'And Alison Duke?'

'Said to be making progress. Physically, that is. They've still not told her the full truth about her mother.'

The Commander stared for a few moments at the typescript. 'Tell me something,' he said. 'What was it put Bob Royce on the scent?'

'One or two things, sir. But chiefly the wig.'

'Which wig?'

'The one found in the garden at the Dukes' house. Bob and I had a discussion about it.' Cullen frowned at the door, assembling his thoughts. 'The thing neither of us could understand was how the bomber had found the time to dispose of the thing right at the back of a dense bush when he was running like the clappers just a few seconds ahead of us. It seemed impossible that he could have done that and still been able to leap the fence at the end of the garden and melt clean away. Well of course, it *was* impossible. And it didn't happen.'

'What did, exactly?'

'I battered my brain over it,' Cullen went on, his steadfast adherence to chronology bringing a grudging smile to the sombre face of the Chief, 'but it was Bob who had the wit to make a few relevant enquiries. What he discovered was that of the three squad cars which had answered the first call to the house, none of them had brought Ferguson. And yet Ferguson was one of the first on the scene. Which was baffling.'

'Was Ferguson asked about it?'

'Until the final episode there hadn't been time to ask him. It was only then that confirmation came through. You remember when you and I were in the waiting room at the hospital and Bob asked to be excused? That was when he put another call through to headquarters and was given the information, which he'd applied for earlier.'

'And the penny dropped?'

'Let's say it tinkled a bit. If Ferguson didn't arrive in one of those cars, Bob argued, wasn't it at least feasible that he was already there at the house?'

'As, of course, he was,' the Chief put in. 'Having been interrupted while attacking the girl, he'd raced through to the back garden, snatched off the wig, dived behind the bush...'

'Hidden the wig,' supplemented Cullen, 'and then crawled back under cover of the other shrubs to the front of the house, where he simply showed himself as Detective-Sergeant Ferguson and joined in the hunt. After that, he had the audacity to 'find' the wig and point it out to Bob. That was a small touch he couldn't resist.'

Following Cullen's eyes towards the report on the desk, the Chief added, 'Merely one of the many touches he just had to apply.'

The Commander flung himself back in his seat. 'There's going to have to be an official enquiry, of course. The Press are already screaming. How did it happen, how could such a man be taken on to the Squad? Frankly, gentlemen, there are still a number of questions I want the answer to myself.' He hesitated. 'One of them has no direct bearing on Ferguson. It concerns police efficiency. Who was supposed to be responsible for searching the basement area at the hospital, and how was it that Ferguson was overlooked?'

'The responsibility was mine, sir.' Cullen spoke quietly. 'He shouldn't have been overlooked. The sole mitigating factor is he had picked a very crafty spot—behind what seemed to be a solid bank of meters at the back of a stair-cupboard half-way down to the boiler-room. There was space behind the lower part of the meter panel, enough to take him if he forced the panel out a foot or so.'

'In a sense,' interposed the Chief, 'your question does have a bearing on Ferguson. It demonstrates the sort of brain we were up against...'

'One accepts,' Asherton said bleakly, 'that he was smart. It doesn't affect the need for an enquiry. Admittedly, his record is good. Army experience, knowledge of explosives, favourable police service report, reputation for tenacity, dedication...the ideal combination, one would have thought. Did nothing of his warped character ever show through?'

The Chief pulled a face. 'His Squad work had been satisfactory, on the whole. Right, Harry?'

Cullen nodded. 'If not quite as brilliant as he liked people to think. He was accepted for what he was...a loner among individualists. As you know, sir, we're granted a good deal of elbow-room on the Squad. It's been found to pay off, the idea being to build up contacts, get results when it counts. Ferguson seemed competent enough at this sort of thing, and now and then he did produce some leads that proved fruitful...'

'No one's denying it,' the Commander said restively.

'In fact, he's had a minor hand in a couple of our major successes. Those where we've hauled in the villains *plus* the material. It's important to bear that in mind.'

'Because Ferguson would have had access to some of that material?'

'Precisely, sir. He didn't need much. Enough for his occasional devices, which in explosive content were quite small.'

Asherton jumped to his feet. 'But *why*?'

Cullen bent his gaze upon the Chief, who coughed and leaned across for the report. 'You'll find some of the answer, I think, in the later stages of this,' he said, turning the sheets with a thumb. 'Without reading slabs out, though, one can summarize a bit. As a preliminary, I can tell you a thing or two from my own observations. From the time he joined the Squad, Ferguson was noted for standing on his dignity...is that the right phrase, Harry? By this I mean, he had a tendency to behave as if the real work was being done by himself while the rest of us toiled after him, picking up the crumbs. Nothing so unusual about that: there's usually someone who reckons he's cock of the roost. In Ferguson's case, though, it made him slightly a figure of fun...'

'He was ribbed about it?'

'Only in the mildest way, sir,' Cullen said firmly. 'What it amounted to was that something about him made people feel disposed to take him down a peg or two. The more he implied by his manner that he was the greatest, the more he invited the snub...and so the more he postured. We've seen it before.'

'The classic vicious circle,' remarked the Chief.

Asherton frowned. 'You knew of this, yourself?'

'Merely as one of a hundred factors concerning the Squad. It didn't seem noticeably serious. Nothing to justify transferring him to other duties. On the contrary, his standard of work was reasonably consistent, and he gave everyone a bit of amusement from time to time.'

'So there was no friction. Except possibly inside himself?'

'Ah,' said the Chief. 'You've got it.'

Cullen said, 'His face never showed a lot. I used to think he was pretty even-tempered in a pompous sort of way. Which just shows once again how deceptive appearances can be.'

'You mean, the somewhat irreverent treatment from his colleagues was cutting deeper than anyone knew? Tipping him over the edge?'

'There was rather more to it than that. What we were seeing were the symptoms, not the causes.'

'Symptoms of what?'

'A lousy boyhood,' said the Chief.

Asherton sighed. 'Don't tell me. He was brought up in an orphanage?'

'Nothing of the kind. He lived at home in a council house in Nottingham and had a doting mother.'

'Then how was it—'

'But he didn't seem happy at school and he didn't do well. Which was something of a mystery, because he was apparently of average intelligence. Later, when he joined the Army, he let slip the reason to a perceptive recruiting officer, who took the trouble to include it in his confidential report. The X-factor was a bullying father.'

'He was knocked about as a lad?'

'Not physically. Worse than that. From the time he started to toddle he was verbally cut to ribbons. His father apparently was a local council clerical worker with a high opinion of himself: he seems to have confidently expected a genius for a son, and when he found that Fate hadn't obliged him...' The Chief brandished an arm.

The Commander sniffed. 'My old man expected a hell of a lot from me.'

'This campaign was pathological. Nothing Ferguson achieved was good enough. The harder he tried, the less he impressed and the more he wanted to impress. He hated and despised his father, and yet all he could think of were ways of proving himself in his eyes, showing what he was made of.'

Asherton regarded the report with a certain beadiness. 'All right,' he said presently, 'he had a swine of a dad. What about the fond mum? Didn't she compensate?'

'She seems to have been a weak, stupid woman. Although she tended to fuss over her son—he was an only child—she never stood up for him against her husband. This is what Ferguson told the recruiting officer...he must have been in a self-exposing mood that day. "She was dead scared of the bastard''—those were the words he used. It's a fair assumption that her behaviour gave him a lifelong contempt for womanhood in general.'

'And so the net result of all this, I take it...'

'The net outcome was an inferiority complex of the worst imaginable kind. It expressed itself in paranoia—an obsession with being top, excelling, outshining everyone around him...'

'I could point,' observed the Commander, 'to a dozen people in this building alone with similar tendencies.'

'But do they all detest the human race?'

'It wouldn't astound me.'

'Ferguson, sir,' said Cullen, who had been silent for a while, 'has not sympathetic feelings of any kind towards his fellow-men. In his mind, they exist simply to be exploited in his own favour.'

'And his fellow-women?'

'They repulse him. He could never have a relationship with a female. Almost certainly he's impotent.'

'So,' said the Commander, returning to his desk from the window-ledge, 'we're left with a male-persecuted, woman-hating, self-glorifying solitary misfit with a working knowledge of explosives. How did this twisted mess come to be welcomed into the Squad and given his head for six years?'

'In retrospect,' the Chief said peevishly, 'it's possible to see how everyone was misled. Taken on face value his various defects looked more like positive advantages. An unmarried man, no ties, no distractions, living apparently for nothing but his work...'

'That's literally true, sir,' Cullen intervened. 'His entire life was geared to the notion of proving himself to the world. Any small success he might have had with the Squad, though, wasn't nearly enough. He had to be the undisputed champ. So there you have the pattern. Basically, Ferguson has always longed to kill his father. But it was easier and almost as satisfying to do it by proxy, by indiscriminate slaughter; with the added attraction that he could then take a leading part in investigating the disasters, and even possibly rig a case against the wrong person and claim kudos for a conviction.

He was playing God.'

For a full minute the Commander sat motionless, glaring into space.

At last he said dully, 'He's having the finest medical attention. Before long, his multiple external injuries are going to be sufficiently patched up to allow him to stand trial, face a posse of shrinks, whatever we decide to do with him. Then he'll be shoved away somewhere, out of harm's way, out of sight, and we'll close the file. What good's it going to do? Who's going to treat his inner deformities?'

The Chief ignited a cigar. 'I'm glad,' he observed through coils of smoke, 'the little nurse survived. But after she was thrown out, it's a pity that damn car didn't burst into flames.'

Royce walked into the sun-room where Trisha was installed with her feet up, intent upon a paperback. His shadow across the page made her look up.

'You're not supposed to be reading,' he said.

Lowering the book, she gave him an exhaustive inspection. 'So that's what you look like.'

'Disappointed?'

'I'm used to shocks. How about you?'

Crouching, he examined the face that she had turned to the light. 'Big improvement on the original, I'd say.'

'Scar-tissue's the rage this season.'

'Next year's the time to think about. They tell me you're going to be as good as new after the plastic surgeon has had his fling. But if you go on staring at small print,' he added, removing the book from her fingers and casting it aside, 'you'll ruin your eyes.'

'You're worse than the nurses,' she complained. 'Not so pretty, either. How's everything on the Squad?'

'Simmering down,' he said briefly. 'When do you leave this place?'

'Day after tomorrow. Home then to Fulham. Nothing exciting like police protection or decoy ruses. Just dreary old housekeeping with the aid of Aunt Polly from Worthing who's moving in for a while. Sorry we never had the chance to work as a team, you and me.'

'You wouldn't have enjoyed it. Tell you what, though. You're going to need protection when you take off from here. From the Press hyenas. Shall I send someone along?'

'A good cop,' she said, 'never delegates.'

Cullen was waiting patiently outside by the car. 'Glad you decided against staying the night,' he remarked. 'I'm in the space reserved for the Hospital Chief Administrator, a tyrant by all accounts. Let's get out of here.' Casually he added, 'Everything okay?'

Royce said thoughtfully, 'She doesn't look bad at all.'

When they were through the hospital gates, he spoke again. 'After she's fixed up, she'll be going back to modelling, she says.'

'Good.' Having negotiated a road junction, Cullen glanced at his companion. 'Sensible idea, yes?'

'Theraputic, possibly.' Royce sounded faraway. 'She's got brains, though. Pity if they went to waste.' A moment later he said, 'She might benefit from a spot of impartial advice.'

Cullen braked courteously at a pedestrian crossing, grinning inanely at its lone user, a middle-aged woman who had gesticulated an acknowledgement. 'Ginny,' he suggested, 'seems full of bright ideas. She's the one, after all, who tipped you off about Ferguson. If that doesn't indicate feminine perception... Why not get her to have a word with Trisha?'

'Ginny doesn't miss a lot,' agreed her brother, looking more alert. 'I'll tell you something. The evening after Ferguson had called to see the rooms she gave me her off-the-cuff analysis of his character —and you know what? She could have lifted most of it straight from that report on Asherton's desk. She ought to have been a psychiatrist. Mind you, she needs her own head examined.'

'Why?' demanded Cullen, concentrating on the traffic.

Royce gave him a sly look. 'She keeps going on about this cop she's got herself stuck with. Can't talk of anything else. Trouble is, he's a rank ahead of me, so I daren't say too much. What's your opinion? Think she's made the right choice?'

The bright crimson of Cullen's face sent him off into snorts of laughter.

Leaning back in the driving seat, Cullen allowed him time to recover.

Presently, with a certain tranquillity, he replied. 'I'd have to make enquiries first. Remind me, will you, Inspector, to run a check on her relatives. These days, you can't be too careful.'

WILBUR SMITH TITLES IN LARGE PRINT

Goldmine

The Diamond Hunters

Eagle in the Sky. (two volumes)

The Eye of The Tiger. (two volumes)

When the Lion Feeds. (two volumes)

The Dark Of The Sun

Shout At The Devil

The Sound of Thunder

ANTONY TREW TITLES IN LARGE PRINT

Death of a Supertanker

Kleber's Convoy

The Moonraker Mutiny

MAIGRET TITLES IN LARGE PRINT

Maigret & The Man on The Boulevard

Maigret & The Spinster

Maigret & The Millionaires

Maigret & The Hotel Majestic

Maigret & The Loner

Maigret & The Black Sheep

Maigret & The Dosser

THE TOFF TITLES IN LARGE PRINT

The Toff & The Stolen Tresses

Model For The Toff

The Toff & The Runaway Bride

The Toff & The Spider

The Toff & The Golden Boy

The Toff & The Fallen Angels

The Toff & The Sleepy Cowboy

The Toff & The Crooked Copper

JAMES HADLEY CHASE TITLES IN LARGE PRINT

The Joker in the Pack

Believe This... You'll Believe Anything

Just Another Sucker

There's a Hippie on the Highway

My Laugh Comes Last

An Ace Up My Sleeve

MICHAEL HARTMAN TITLES IN LARGE PRINT

Game for Vultures

Leap for the Sun

Shadow of the Leopard

LARGE TYPE EDITION